MY CHEMICAL MOUNTAIN

MY CHEMICAL MOUNTAIN

Corina Vacco

delacorte press

Text copyright © 2013 by Corina Vacco
Jacket photograph copyright © 2013 by Shane Rebenschied

All rights reserved. Published in the United States by Delacorte Press,
an imprint of Random House Children's Books,
a division of Random House, Inc., New York.

Delacorte Press is a registered trademark and the colophon
is a trademark of Random House, Inc.

Visit us on the Web! randomhouse.com/teens

Educators and librarians, for a variety of teaching tools, visit us at
RHTeachersLibrarians.com

Library of Congress Cataloging-in-Publication Data
Vacco, Corina.
My chemical mountain / Corina Vacco. — 1st ed.
p. cm.
Summary: The summer before they begin high school, best friends Jason,
Charlie, and Cornpup go after the chemical plant that has been polluting
their town, one seeking revenge for his father's death and
the others mainly for the thrill of it.
ISBN 978-0-385-74242-9 (hc) — ISBN 978-0-307-97504-1 (ebook)
[1. Pollution—Fiction. 2. Conduct of life—Fiction. 3. Best friends—Fiction.
4. Friendship—Fiction. 5. Environmentalism—Fiction. 6. Vigilantes—Fiction.
7. Death—Fiction. 8. Compulsive eating—Fiction.] I. Title.
PZ7.V15My 2013
[Fic]—dc23   2012030550

The text of this book is set in 12-point Goudy.
Book design by Kenny Holcomb

Printed in the United States of America

10 9 8 7 6 5 4 3 2

First Edition

For my beautiful mother:
activist, artist, cultivator of imagination.
I love you.

CHAPTER 1
CRASH

THE wind carries sulfur and hard rain. Power lines are down in the streets. I trace the outline of a petroleum serpent on my foggy window and wipe it away with my fist. I think about the seventeen tons of Phenzorbiflux that went missing the night Dad died. Green, steamy chemical sludge. Coveralls in a puddle of liquefied human skin. The horrible phone call that woke us in the night. I am hungry for revenge.

Last time there was a storm like this, me and Charlie hot-wired a dump truck and crashed it into the field of barrels. The time before that we started a small chemical fire in the creek, watched the water burn in the rain. Storms make us wild sometimes, like animals.

Mom calls to me from the kitchen. "Jason, where are you? Can you *believe* how bad it's raining? I wish you wouldn't hide away in your room all night. Come help me fold towels." I can tell she's eating something from one of her stashes. She has hidden bags of cheese curls in the coat closet, pork rinds under an end table in the living room, chocolate-covered pretzels in a Christmas tin in the garage. Eating is her new tic, like a twitching eye or a stutter.

There is an explosion of thunder, the kind that sounds like it's right on top of you, or maybe even *inside* you, and then my room goes dark. The ceiling fan stops spinning. The television blinks off. Charlie's gonna be here any minute now. It's just a matter of time.

Mom taps on my door. "It looks like you're off the hook. I have a feeling the power'll be out for the rest of the night. I'm going to bed." She can be disgusting sometimes, spilling chunky beef soup down the front of her pajamas, falling asleep with potato chips in her mouth. I wonder what it feels like to wake up every morning as her—thirsty and still tired, crumbs on the pillow case, swollen fingers.

Charlie, where are you?

I lie on my bed and listen for cars on the 990. I have a short dream about blue spiders in an underground cave. Something rattles my bedroom window. My eyes snap open. My stomach is pulsing like a machine, painful pistons and gears. There is a siren in the distance. I grab an old sweatshirt and climb out my window. Slowly, silently.

Charlie is standing next to his dad's new four-wheeler. It is blue and black with a wolf custom-painted on the front. It smells like gasoline and vinyl. We aren't supposed to go near it.

"Think Randy can airbrush something like that onto my dirt bike?" I say. The rain is falling hard, like gravel on my face.

Charlie just looks at me. Maybe he notices the stains on my jeans: black spray paint and battery acid on the knees, mud everywhere else. Or maybe he's looking right through me, his mind kicking around some kind of trouble at home.

"What's *your* problem?" I ask. He's seemed distracted a lot this summer, but the circles under his eyes are new.

He blinks and says, "I can't sleep. I'm so tired, I'm not even tired."

"I'm never tired," I say. "I only sleep because it's boring to stay up forever."

Already my sweatshirt is wet and heavy. Charlie has on army-green rubber boots and a pair of welder's goggles. I consider the black garbage bags we have in the garage, how easy it would be to turn them into raincoats.

Charlie's scars look blue in the lightning. I sit on the back of the four-wheeler as he steers us away from our neighborhood. We take the old steel bridge across Two Mile Creek. We jump flooded ditches and skid onto empty highways. I lift my face to the sky and drink the rain. I taste motor oil on my lips.

The Poxton landfill looms up ahead, black and eerie on the horizon. Charlie calls it Chemical Mountain. To him it is one of the wonders of the world. If we could spend every moment there, jumping barrels on our dirt bikes or racing snowmobiles, he'd be happy. Cornpup, though, he calls our landfill the Nightmare. He spits on it, pees on it, swears at it—like a mound of chemicals and dirt can have hurt feelings or whatever. He hammers toxicity reports to his wall and says words like *uranium*, then watches our faces for a reaction.

When we pull up to Chemical Mountain, lightning strikes a nearby tree. My skin is buzzing.

Charlie kills the engine. "When I come here, I feel real strong," he says. "Like I could pull down a bunch of electric wires and not get shocked. Like I could pick up a cement truck and throw it across a field."

"I still think we should bottle the dirt, sell it," I say. Then I feel stupid, because Charlie would never give away his secret. He eats handfuls of mud from Chemical Mountain. He swallows orange and green water from Two Mile Creek. He's the only fourteen-year-old in Poxton who can catch a thirty-yard pass in triple coverage. His muscles are like steel coils under his skin. I'd eat anything to be like that, but I tried it once, and all I got was a rash of hot blisters on my tongue.

Thunder rips through the sky.

There is a chain-link fence at the base of Chemical Mountain. Charlie pitches rocks at the NO TRESPASSING signs while I pry open the gate with his crowbar. We ride to the top of our landfill, lightning all around us, the air so electric I feel dizzy. I squint because the rain is falling sideways, straight at our faces. From the summit we look down on a large rectangle of darkness—our street and the neighboring streets, still without power—and we feel like war gods, like we've conquered something for real.

"Drive fast," I shout to Charlie.

As if he has to be told.

We fly down Chemical Mountain at full throttle. I think about how, two weeks ago, Mom missed my eighth-grade graduation. I came home to find her sitting on the kitchen floor, eating fried hamburger out of a casserole pan, holding her spoon like a shovel. I grabbed her ceramic turtle from the windowsill and smashed it against the tile. I would've broken more than just a turtle if Charlie hadn't walked in. He swept up the mess, and Mom belched silently, and I wanted to pack a suitcase and take off. Except I don't have anyplace to go.

The thing is, she wasn't like that when Dad was alive.

My nose is bleeding again. I don't like to bleed the way Charlie likes to bleed. It's not a badge of honor to me. I wipe the blood on my sleeve. Neither of us thinks about the large metal vents that release gases from the landfill's belly. We want the rush, the thrill of speeding without limits, without lights, without anyone to stop us.

Halfway down the mountain, I hear a horrible sound, like a chain saw cutting through steel. The four-wheeler flips and rolls. I fly twenty feet, and my shoulder pops when I hit the ground. Pain

4

shoots through me, but I do not cry out. There's mud in my eyes. I hear Charlie shouting—"*Are you okay? Are you okay? Are you okay?*" It's so like him to injure his wrist and ignore it, to worry about me instead. I don't tell him I landed next to a damaged vent that's reaching up through the weeds like a tiny sword. I think about the sandwiches at Tavern on the Creek. White bread and turkey and tomato and cheese with a toothpick stabbed straight through the middle.

That could've been me.

We stand over the ruins of the four-wheeler for a long time. The custom-painted wolf is crunched up, all that detail, just . . . gone. Dark liquid is dripping from the engine. Charlie is jamming his fist into his thigh, like he's already formulating a plan. He says he's gonna mess up the garage and make it look like a burglary, like the four-wheeler got stolen. I don't understand how he will explain his swollen wrist.

"You worry too much," he says.

We take a bold shortcut home, trespassing on Mareno Chem's property, knowing that if we get caught, they'll press charges. The parking lot is empty except for a shiny silver Lexus. A slimy liar owns that car. I wish I had the guts to slash his tires. Or worse.

We enter mudflat territory. It's hard to walk with the ground sucking at our shoes. I lead Charlie up and over a rugged, uncapped landfill, which is a mistake, because he finds a dead red-tailed hawk, its wings all soggy, and he makes me dig a hole in the wet garbage with his crowbar so we can give the bird a real burial. Just beyond the landfill is our high school. The sight of it makes me want to puke my guts out.

Charlie says, "See the football field? That's all fresh turf they've got there. I'm gonna get new cleats before tryouts. I've been real disciplined about saving my money."

High school will be easy for Charlie, because everyone likes him—plus he's a badass football player. High school will probably be easy for Cornpup too, because he's the type who doesn't care what people think, and there's so much freedom in that. I'm the one who's scared. I'm the one who's not ready. What if me and my friends drift apart in a big school? We could end up in different classes or get swallowed by totally opposite groups of friends. I feel the end of summer chasing me, snapping its jaws at my heels.

"I'm starving," says Charlie. "I have to eat soon or I'm gonna die."

Charlie's dad can bust holes through a wooden door with his bare hands. One firecracker snap of his leather belt and you're bleeding. It's the whisky. It's the economy. It's always something.

"Your old man's gonna kill you when he finds out you destroyed the four-wheeler. You can crash on my floor tonight if you want."

"He won't find out. I've got it covered," Charlie says, spitting blood into a puddle. "Anyway, my mom went shopping after work. We've got blueberry waffles in the freezer."

Later, maybe tomorrow, Cornpup will yell at us for not dragging the four-wheeler home. He will walk all the way to Chemical Mountain to examine the twisted machine. He'll fill a giant duffel bag with things that mean nothing to Charlie and me: hinges, strut springs, cables and belts, rotary valve parts, and a motor mount. It'll take him weeks, and it won't be pretty—bodywork is needed, and a new paint job—but he'll get the four-wheeler running again, its motor purring like new. I give him credit for seeing potential where I see only a hopeless mess. I wish he knew how to bring people back to life.

It's not fair that my dad, a man who wouldn't even plug in a table saw without safety gloves, is dead. He was a drummer and football player. He followed the rules. He picked up some overtime hours at the chemical processing plant, just wanted some extra cash, and now they say the accident was his fault. Being good didn't get him anywhere. Playing it safe didn't earn him extra points. He could've been a skydiver or a junkie or a stuntman. It wouldn't've mattered.

Charlie says it's hard for kids to die, that it's almost *impossible*, but I saw Joe Farley the day he puked all over the Pelliteros' sidewalk. He'd gone swimming in Two Mile Creek when the water smelled like melted plastic, and anyone with half a brain knows that the colored water is fine, that it's the smelly water you have to stay away from. His eyes were all bloodshot. I asked him if he was okay, and he said I should "piss off." Later that day he fell from the window of the abandoned rubber factory on Grant Street. I've been in the building with Charlie a million times, but we were always smart enough to kick open the warehouse doors. We would never go up the fire escape and in through the windows, because there's no way to climb down the fifty-foot walls once you're inside. You have to jump to an old catwalk and catch a ladder that way, which is probably how the Farley kid fell. It's not an easy jump to make. Only Charlie has done it, and even he says, *Never again*.

Before I hoist myself through my bedroom window, Charlie says, "Mareno Chem reopened their drainage pipes. They're dumping in the creek again."

"Cornpup's gonna be so pissed," I say. And we both laugh.

Dumping.

To me it's maintenance, like taking out the garbage or getting a haircut. No big deal. To Charlie it's what keeps us real; it's what separates us from the hybrid car–driving wimps who couldn't hold on to a football if their hands were covered in epoxy.

But a few months ago, Cornpup started to really freak out. He said our creek was all poisoned or whatever. He took horsehair blankets and insulation from his attic and clogged up Mareno Chem's drainage pipes while me and Charlie played football on the muddy shore. We told him his plug wouldn't hold, but he wasn't trying to stop the sludge forever. He was just sending a message. "I don't

7

want them to think we're stupid, that we don't notice what's been going on," he told us. Then Charlie threw the football hard, and sure as shit, it bounced off Cornpup's hands and into the water. It was hilarious.

There is another rip of thunder, then a flash of lightning so close and bright, we both stop laughing. Charlie lifts the welder's goggles from his face. "Oh, one more thing. I think I know where they're hiding the Phenzorbiflux."

He says he'll show me where. Tomorrow night. He says some other stuff too. But I can't hear him anymore. The monster is back inside my head, pounding on my skull. I can feel a bad migraine coming on. Sometimes I wonder about my anger, how long it can be controlled.

CHAPTER 2
ADRENALINE

THE day after a lightning storm, I sometimes get headaches, like the ones we all got the year our school was closed down because noxious gasses were coming up through the basement vents. My shoulder is still sore from the crash at Chemical Mountain, but if Charlie's telling the truth, if he really found the Phenzorbiflux barrels, there's *no way* I'm staying home tonight.

Mom picked up an early Saturday shift at the plant. She left me a note on the table—*Stay away from the creek*—which makes me laugh, because she has no right to tell me that. Two Mile Creek is the heartbeat of our whole summer. It's where we find tumor-covered snakes and two-headed robins. It's where Charlie invented water football and you have to jump into a huge pile of rusted metal to get a touchdown. When Cornpup built a crazy-fast boat out of aluminum siding, a busted carousel horse, and a junk motor that runs on chicken grease, Two Mile Creek was where we first took it for a spin.

Two Mile Creek is *ours*.

I lie on the couch and watch *Rocky III*, the good one, where he loses to Clubber Lang, and then I cook some tomato soup with cut-up hot dogs. My headache goes away once I have food in my stomach. I'm bored, though. There's nothing else good on TV.

I walk to the creek because I want to see if the water is still the color of antifreeze, and because I want to sculpt creatures out of heavy mud and pieces of broken glass, and because Mom is stupid if she thinks she can keep me away from Two Mile with a note.

The humidity today is almost unbearable. My thirsty pores drink in the steamy chemical fumes that blow in off Lake Erie. At the edge of the industrial park, I scale a chain-link fence. I walk along a footpath of garbage, plastic mostly—huge, crushed-up tubs that smell like gasoline. When I finally reach the creek, my head is foggy. I swear I can almost hear how this place must've sounded a hundred years ago, when all the factory machines were humming, before everything got shut down.

There's an orange film on the creek. I drag a stick through the water, breaking up the color as I walk, but the suds come together again real quick, like a wound healing. Colored water is so much cooler than regular old murky creek water, but there are people—like Mom and Cornpup—who say it's toxic. They want the creek fenced off. Me and Charlie, we'll fight them every step of the way.

I hang at the creek for about an hour, wading in the water, fishing out golf balls, carving images in the mud with a long piece of glass, until I see a guy in a yellow plastic suit collecting water samples in long glass tubes. I nod at him, just being friendly or whatever, and he says, "Get out of the frickin' water. What are you, crazy?" which is totally uncalled for. Then he leaves.

I'm about to walk home, when Charlie shows up. No bruises on his face, which means he didn't get blamed for the four-wheeler. "Your shoes are garbage," he says.

Like I don't know this. I've been taping them up for months.

Charlie climbs a dead tree, swings from the highest branch, and does a cannonball into the orange, fizzy water. I'm already up the tree when he surfaces for air. I crawl out to the end of a branch, swing by my hands for a minute, and then let go. I try doing a somersault in the air, but I don't have enough momentum, so instead I do a belly flop that hurts. Charlie laughs at me. I go under and drink in a mouthful of water to spit into his face. He spits back at me. We go back and forth for a while, like water dragons battling it out. My throat is burning. His eyes are bloodshot.

The afternoon sun turns the water a darker color, almost tomato-red. I'm ready to do something else.

"So what's up with you and Valerie?" Charlie asks me.

"Nothing."

"Bull."

"She called. I wasn't home. That's it." But that's not it. I like her. A lot.

We use empty glass jars to dig for Cornpup's robots, but we don't find them. Cornpup is real paranoid when it comes to his inventions. He has a secret map of hiding spots. What we do find is his metal detector wrapped in a blue tarp. Charlie uses it to look for machine parts buried deep in the ground like bones. I fill the glass jars with some deformed tadpoles and weird insects, stuff Cornpup can use for the Freak Museum.

"Kind of looks like a purple spider." I show Charlie the rash that's forming on my forearm.

"Mine are better," Charlie says. He's got snakelike scales on both ankles.

We head back for food. Charlie has a corroded battery tucked under his arm. He loves corroded stuff. Before we part ways, he says, "We're going out to the yards at midnight. I'll come get you. Be ready."

"Yeah, yeah. I'll be ready."

Mom's home when I get back. She's already wolfed down a frozen pizza, didn't even leave me one slice. On the table there's a stack of opened mail, mostly bills. I'm drawn to a letter that's printed on Army Corps of Engineers letterhead. I skim it, my eyes snagging on certain words:

> . . . Two Mile Creek . . . discharge pipes . . . immediate threat . . . Mareno Chem . . . highly toxic azo dyes . . . not to panic . . . surrounding areas . . . assessing the risk . . . not for recreational use . . .

"Why do you have this?" I say.

Mom points a fat finger at me. "Two Mile Creek is a mess. They say it might not be possible to clean up all the poison. They're talking about fencing it off. I think it's a good idea."

I'm so mad, I want to punch something. "What about me? What about my summer? They're taking everything away from us."

It's like I can't hold on to anything.

I picture a bunch of sweaty construction workers digging holes, installing aluminum fence posts, puncturing our tunnels, confiscating our fireworks and crowbars, destroying Cornpup's robots and throwing away the busted metal pieces.

Mom shrugs. "You told me the creek has dead frogs all up and down the banks. That's not normal. And the dyes in the water. I remember when I had to use a Brillo pad to get oily red stains off your skin after you went swimming there."

"Me and Charlie swim there all the time, and we're fine."

Mom rolls her eyes. "Just stop. You *know* what I think about

12

Charlie. He's a bad seed. His whole family is nothing but trash. He'll jump the fence, and you'll follow. I swear if that boy jumped off the Skyway, you'd be right behind him."

Her words sting me like the phosphorus rocks we found in a corroded railcar near our old middle school. Strangers can make snap judgments about me all day long. I don't care. But when my own mom does it, it hurts. She thinks I follow Charlie, like I'm not my own person, but I spend lots of time drawing, and Charlie would never sit still that long. I created the baddest sketchbook full of landfill monsters. And last time I checked, I'm not going out for football, even though Charlie's been begging. Sometimes I think Mom doesn't know me at all. I could die in a few hours, could get crushed under a steel beam. But at least I'll have discovered something more interesting than potato chips. At least I know what it feels like to be alive.

I open the refrigerator and stare at the shelves. A jug of milk. Polish sausages. Liverwurst. American cheese. Mostaccioli. Nothing looks good.

I remember how much trouble I got in back before Cornpup scored formaldehyde for our Freak Museum. It had been my stupid idea to take all the crazy stuff we found on the shores of Two Mile and store it in my kitchen. Wingless birds in a margarine tub in the freezer. Neon-green leeches wrapped in foil and hidden in the silverware drawer. A big fish with tumors on its face in a plastic bag behind the ice maker. Mom found the dead animals a few days later, and I got double-grounded, no contact with friends for a week.

I sneer at her now. "Where's my BLT?"

"Your what?"

"The BLT I got at Joe's Roadhouse on Thursday night. Did you eat it?"

"I . . . um . . . I don't think so."

"You don't remember if you ate my food? Are you serious?"

"I don't want to fight with you." She folds up the letter and shoves it into her purse with such force that her glass of soda tips over and spills everywhere. She looks like she wants to burst out crying. I almost help her wipe up the mess, but something holds me back. I'm still kind of pissed at what she said about Charlie—he's not a bad seed; he's loyal and funny. The real bad seed is the slimy Mareno Chem lawyer who harassed us after Dad's funeral. And Mom was so quick to cut a deal with him: total silence in exchange for a few hundred dollars. Charlie would never sell out like that.

I never signed any papers. I never agreed to be silent. The only vow I took was in my own head. Revenge.

CHAPTER 3
SNEAKING OUT

IT'S after midnight and Charlie's still not here.

Outside, one of our neighbors is stuck in the mud. I hear tires spinning. I remember a few winters ago, when Dad's van got buried in a snowy parking lot. We threw down salt to melt the ice and poured kitty litter under the tires for traction. He told me to sit in the driver's seat and "floor it" while he pushed. It took us thirty minutes to get unstuck. I remember thinking Dad was strong for pushing a huge van without any help. But really, pushing stuck vehicles is just a thing people do. You don't have to be all that powerful.

I smear butter in a pan and fry up some bologna. Mom must smell the food, because she wanders into the kitchen and says, "Whatcha making?" When she thinks I'm not looking, she takes a box of ice cream sandwiches and hides it in the laundry basket under a pile of towels. She says, "I'm going to put on a movie and fold the rest of these in my bedroom." She touches my face.

"What?" I say.

She puts her arms around me. "I just love you."

I'm stiff in her embrace, but she keeps holding me, and I feel myself relaxing. She is my only parent. She's my *mom*. I don't put my arms around her, though. I won't hug her back.

"Good night," she whispers.

I eat the fried bologna straight from the pan. Mom disappears into her bedroom, her little TV drowning out the sound of an ice cream box tearing open. She's gonna eat the whole box in one sitting. Those ice cream sandwiches were supposed to be for both of us.

I sit on the couch and wrap masking tape around my sneakers until I'm certain they'll hold. I jump a little when Charlie taps on the mudroom window with his crowbar. I open the front door and say, "Be really quiet. My mom just went to bed."

"Look what I did to my hand," Charlie says. His straight blond hair is ratted from the wind.

Cornpup is here too. He sets a paper bag on my floor. I wonder what's in it. "You look like a death row inmate," I tell him.

"Shut up. I like my hair short."

We haven't been out to the abandoned factories since November, not all three of us, anyway. Charlie is always outside, until his lips crack from the wind, and I can be indoors or out, it doesn't matter, but as soon as the temperature drops below fifty, Cornpup sits on the floor vent in his living room, cranks the heat up to a million degrees, and reads stacks of books from the library. We barely see him between January and May. His health is bad, that's why. The skin on his arms is thin, like sausage casing. The nodules on his back have a limited blood supply, and when he's really cold, they turn a waxy white color that makes me think of navy beans from a can.

Charlie says, "We found a way into the grain mill. The Mareno Chem trucks are parked inside."

They cased the mill without me. No wonder they took so long to get here.

"We didn't go in yet," Charlie adds. "We came back to get you first." When he smiles, he raises his hand to cover his teeth. He'll have to do that for the rest of his life, probably. Last summer, when he was riding on the back of his brother's motorcycle, they got into an accident on Military Road. Randy had road rash all down his back, but he healed quickly, with no scars. Charlie was the one who had lasting damage. He banged his skull on the pavement and lost two of his teeth. His parents still don't know because he always covers his mouth when he chews or smiles. After the accident, when the rubber skid marks were still fresh, we rode our bikes out to the scene. Charlie wanted to find his teeth. He was gonna make them into a necklace or something. I found a tiger's-eye agate, and he found a long piece of dried snakeskin, but we didn't find the teeth.

"It stinks bad outside. Worse than when the asphalt plant caught fire," says Cornpup. Before he closes the door, I catch a glimpse of the gray and orange night sky, summer fog mixed with vomiting smokestacks. Past the Kuperskis' house, beyond our school and the ball field, I see a seventy-foot wall of black—Chemical Mountain, with its monster slopes, a hundred boarded-up factories in its valleys.

Charlie's hand is dripping blood all over the floor. "Can I get a pop?" he asks me. "I'm dying of thirst." He always uses that word, *dying.*

"We gotta wrap your hand first," I tell him. "You're getting blood everywhere."

We clamber into the bathroom. Charlie rummages through our medicine cabinet. He says, "How can you not have Band-Aids? Everyone has Band-Aids." Then he pours rubbing alcohol onto his cut and hisses at the pain. He wraps his hand in gauze and tape till it looks like the sneakers I just rigged. He has messed everything up. Cough syrup, dental floss, and lozenges litter the sink. I see one of Dad's old pill bottles—it's unbearable, the places in this house where I can still find pieces of him. I stand here, almost two years after his death, with a sick sadness in my gut, an *aching*, and I wonder if I'll ever feel all right again.

Cornpup doesn't want to carry his paper bag all the way to the grain mill. He says, "Hey, do you have a backpack I can borrow?"

I say no, which isn't the truth. I have one under my bed, but it's filled with railroad spikes.

"Did Charlie tell you he's going to climb the grain elevator?" Cornpup asks me. "He wants to fall and splatter on the floor like that Joe Farley kid."

Charlie makes a face. "The thing about Farley is that he wasn't strong enough to grab the catwalk. I don't have that problem."

We watch Charlie roll up his pants legs. Randy's jeans are still too long for him. I feel jealous, because I notice that Randy has drawn pictures of scorpions above the knees, black ink on denim, and Charlie doesn't even know how cool that is. He always gets to borrow Randy's stuff: steel-toed boots, a wallet with a chain, his silver rattlesnake ring. I should have an older brother. I would appreciate it more.

Once, when I was sitting on the Pelliteros' porch waiting for Charlie to get home, Randy had his acoustic guitar and he taught me a song. I didn't want to leave that porch step, but when the mosquitoes got bad, I went home and drew a set of guitar frets in my sketchbook. I practiced that chord progression for hours, my fingers pressed to the paper.

Tonight, it's my turn. I'm gonna wear something no one else gets to wear. I go to the closet where Mom stored all Dad's favorite belongings—his drumsticks and his autographed Sabres tickets and his Las Vegas beer mug. Charlie helps me pull the fattest box down from a shelf. I slice through the packing tape with a pizza cutter.

Cornpup says, "Are you sure you want to dig through all that stuff tonight?"

I take off my ugly sweatshirt and toss it to the floor. "This'll take two seconds. The thing I'm looking for is real easy to find."

When I see Dad's leather jacket, I feel like I breathed in a bad chemical for too long. The jacket is still shaped like him, still smells like him. He never played a gig without it, even on hot summer nights by the river when the rest of the band members wore T-shirts with the sleeves ripped off. On the back of the jacket, there's an image of a drum set burned into the leather with a branding iron. People always wanted to know where he got a custom jacket like this, who made it for him, but he would never tell.

"Your dad was such a ridiculously good drummer," says Charlie. "That jacket was famous in this town."

I remember the night Dad's band played at the pig roast. Everyone stopped eating during the drum solo, because they were, like, hypnotized. Dad stood up afterward, his back to the crowd, his drumsticks pointing to the sky. I wanted to be onstage with him.

"Don't wear that to the mill," says Cornpup. "It'll get dirty."

"Screw that," says Charlie. "Wear it."

I am already wearing it. The leather hangs heavy on my arms.

Charlie starts rummaging through the cardboard box, like this is a garage sale. He pulls out the switchblade Dad got at a gift shop in Niagara Falls.

"Put it back," I say.

Charlie shakes his head. "No. We might need protection tonight. I'm serious."

I have a sick feeling in my stomach.

We sneak out the back door like burglars. No coughing, no breathing, no nervous laughter.

We don't make a sound.

CHAPTER 4
TRESPASSING

THE industrial zone covers about ten square miles, from Cornpup's backyard to the interstate. First there is a chain-link fence, then an acre of land where plants don't grow, then a field full of partially buried metal barrels. About a hundred factories and mills, most of them closed down and falling apart, form rings around Chemical Mountain, like moons orbiting a planet. Two Mile Creek begins at the mudflats and snakes its way through everything, even traveling *underneath* some of the smaller landfills, which is really cool to see. Lots of buildings got built on the shores of Two Mile Creek. There is a mile-long steel mill; there are factories that manufacture film and rubber and tools and fiberglass and tires; there is an asphalt plant that burned down, an incinerator that's all boarded up, and a bunch of silos that look like castle towers from a distance. Mareno Chem is one of only about twenty-five buildings still in operation.

I want to ask Cornpup what's in the paper bag, but even more than that, I want to ask him why I should even have to ask, why he hasn't told me. Instead I say, "I hope this frickin' tape doesn't fall off my shoes."

Hidden within the industrial zone are secret places only me and my friends know about: a trail of green puddles that never dry up; a rusty railcar full of weird, smelly rocks; and a perfect square of earth where you can dig for hours without seeing a single insect, not even a worm. My favorite thing to look at is the cluster of trees that turned black and died for no reason. When I draw sludge demons in my sketchbook, I usually put those trees in the background.

There is a strange taste in the back of my throat: burnt plastic, natural gas, and a sharp chemical that makes me lose my breath for a second. My throat feels itchy. I can't stop coughing.

"Told you it smells bad out tonight," says Cornpup.

Charlie is up ahead of us, sprinting. He runs through the tall grass like he's found some path no one else can see. Cornpup and I exchange a look. We are supposed to be going to the grain mill together. Charlie is leaving us behind.

We are three-way best friends. We've known each other since we were four years old. There was a time when we all grew at exactly the same rate, and a small part of me liked the fairness in that, liked things being even. Charlie's growth spurt was like an explosion. He was suddenly taller, with chiseled arms, a stomach hard as steel, and a noticeably deeper voice. Pretty girls started doodling his name on their book covers, dotting their i's with little hearts. It made me want to puke. I do okay with the ladies. I've got really dark brown eyes, almost black, and they're shaped like wolf eyes. It's hard for girls to look away from me when I make eye contact. I just wish I wasn't so skinny. At least I don't look like Cornpup—transparent skin, purple nodules on his back, and a messed-up buzz cut. He'll never get a girl.

21

I'm running through the mud like a clumsy idiot. Cornpup is beside me, panting like a dog. "Slow down!" he shouts in his wheezy voice, but there's no way Charlie can hear him.

And then we see Charlie fall.

He has tripped on a rusty piece of machinery that lay hidden beneath the mud. Or he has slipped on a sheen of spilled oil. It's so great to see *him* look stupid for once.

I shout, "That was the best thing I ever saw in my life!"

And Cornpup shouts, "Charlie, you are such a retard!"

Charlie starts running again. I can tell he's embarrassed.

I remember the night Dad organized a winter football game in the middle of Cardinal Drive. Dad was our team's quarterback, of course, and he wanted me to be his receiver, which I should not have agreed to do. We played against Sid Kuperski's son, Jeff, who quarterbacked in college at Syracuse, and Charlie, who was involved in every play, alternating between tight end and linebacker. The snow didn't get in his eyes when he was supposed to make an important catch. The wet ball didn't slip out of his hands like a catfish. I could feel Dad comparing me to Charlie, who was showing off.

And I didn't like it.

I went inside and took out my sketchbook. No one came looking for me. I drew a picture of a giant ice monster throwing a football at Charlie and knocking his head off. I drew the same monster stepping on Dad and crushing him under its foot. But if I could rewind, I would've spent more time with Dad, even if it meant hugging a cold football to my chest and growling like an animal in the end zone.

The lights along the railroad tracks are busted from last night's lightning storm. We pass a field full of moss-covered dump trucks and CSX railcars that from a distance look like lines of beasts. We pass by one of Cornpup's underground tunnels, where Charlie hid our most dangerous fireworks and a pair of dragon nunchucks. We can't see Charlie anymore, but we've walked to the grain mill many times. We've stood before its rusting, crumbling body, its windows that are all covered in spray paint, the hollow shell of a building that was once full of workers and sweet-smelling grain. We could find the mill with our eyes closed, and tonight we will almost have to.

"I saw pirated footage of the Gulf oil spill online," says Corn-pup. "There was this sickening green dispersant in the water. When it caught fire, seabirds were dropping dead out of the sky. Some cleanup workers were hospitalized for melting skin. Sounds like Phenzorbiflux to me."

"The FDA never approved it," I say numbly. "Mareno Chem says Phenzorbiflux doesn't even exist. Kind of a stretch to say they poured it into the Gulf without anyone noticing."

"That's just it." Cornpup is breathing so loudly, I have to strain to understand him. "Maybe"—*wheeze*—"the barrels aren't even here anymore." *Wheeze.* "Maybe they put Phenzorbiflux"—*wheeze*—"in one of the containers"—*wheeze*—"marked for a different dispersant." *Wheeze.* "Maybe they hid it in plain sight."

"No," I say. "It's here. And we're gonna find it. We have to."

Cornpup has me hold his paper bag for a second. He takes his inhaler from his pocket. I watch him suck in the medicine, his eyes closing as his face relaxes. I wonder what it feels like to have your airways swell shut and then reopen. He has to fight for oxygen, which is everywhere and costs nothing. Without that inhaler, he would die. It is stupid for him to be out on a night like this, but I don't say anything. The paper bag has metal cylinders inside it— I've figured out that much—and then Cornpup snatches it back from me.

"Okay. We can run again," he says.

It takes us another five minutes to reach the mill.

"You guys are so friggin' slow," says Charlie.

"We saw you fall," says Cornpup.

Charlie smirks. "You're talking trash *to me?* You, with your ugly purple rashes and your freaky skin? That takes some balls."

Cornpup looks down at the Pabst Blue Ribbon cans by our feet. Charlie shouldn't've brought up the bumps. We've seen what Cornpup has been through—liquid nitrogen and scalpels and bandages. The bumps keep coming back. He doesn't take his shirt off when it's hot out, not even to swim. Cornpup is always saying stuff like "I'm a monster" and "I'm never gonna find a girlfriend" and "I look like a dragon." I never know how to respond. Sometimes I remind him that at least he gets to work a sweet money angle. He charges kids a dollar if they want to see his back, and so far he's saved up enough to buy himself a new Sabres jersey. He's lucky in a way, because Charlie and I could never come up with that kind of cash.

"You aren't supposed to bring up the bumps," I say to Charlie.

He pretends not to hear me. He examines a jagged corner of sheet metal. "Here's where I cut my hand. My blood's on this, see?" He pulls the metal away. The hole in the wall is a tight fit, but it's definitely, *finally,* a way in.

"See you losers on the other side." Charlie slips through the cracked wall so quickly, it is hard to believe he was ever here to begin with.

"I hate when he gets like this," I say to Cornpup. "It makes me want to go home."

Cornpup shakes his head. "I came here to do something. I'm not going back till it's done."

I hear howling in the distance, a dog or a wolf.

Charlie's voice echoes from inside the building. "Are you coming or what?"

Cornpup climbs through the wall. I follow him, careful not to scratch up Dad's leather jacket. I don't feel the adrenaline rush I was expecting. Something about this night is all wrong. Charlie is

24

being mean, and Cornpup is being secretive, and they aren't getting along, which sticks me in the middle.

"There's a cat skeleton over there," says Charlie.

"Stop shining the flashlight at the windows," I say to him.

The industrial zone is divided into quadrants, each patrolled by its own security guard. The amount of land each guard has to cover is unreasonably large. There's no chance in hell they'll find us here, *unless* we do something to catch their attention.

"Wouldn't it be cool if the roof caved in and we had to dig our way out of here?" says Charlie.

"Not really," says Cornpup.

We are surrounded by wooden scaffolding and cold steel beams. I can smell mold and grease and rat poop. The metal machinery—what's left of it—is caked in a thick layer of dust that makes me think of wool blankets. We get scared for a second when a trapped bird flutters its wings desperately against a window thirty feet above us, just below the ceiling. There is no telling how that bird got in here. Or if it will ever escape. I pick up a rock and try to throw it up to the window, but I don't even get close.

"I'll bust that window on my first try," says Charlie. And he does.

The bird flies away from the window at the sound of shattering glass.

"That was worth the effort," says Cornpup.

"Wait," I say. "Give it a second."

We stare through the window frame at our one clear view of the night sky. The bird must feel the pressure change, must smell freedom, because it flies right out the window and into the night. We feel good about ourselves then. The tension between Charlie and Cornpup seems to vanish.

"This place smells like hell," says Cornpup.

"Rat poison," I tell him. "Breathe through your nose."

With every step, there is loud crunching under my shoes. Charlie's rubber boots make squishy sounds when they strike the concrete.

Cornpup says, "Tell us a story, Jason. Something scary."

"Something bloody," says Charlie.

"I can't think of anything right now," I tell them.

Charlie sighs loudly.

"I mean, the story I'm thinking of isn't bloody, because there isn't any blood when you fall into a vat of molten steel. You just kind of turn into human soup."

Human soup. Just like Dad.

"Who fell?" says Cornpup.

"A foreman named Ted. His right eye was made of glass. He got really mad at his workers over the lamest things. He stabbed a pencil through a man's hand over a lost time card. If he caught people talking on the job, he burned their arms on the blast furnaces."

The flashlight goes out. Charlie knocks it twice against a metal drum. The light comes on again, brighter than before.

"Ted chased this worker named Donnie up a catwalk and tried to choke him for clocking in late. Only he didn't know Donnie was a boxer. They started sparring, and Donnie tried to take it easy on his boss, because, you know, it was his *boss*. He didn't want to get canned."

We walk deep into the building, following Charlie like he's a tour guide. I hit my hand on something that then falls to the floor with a crash. I hear rodents squeaking, running away. I wonder what a rat bite would feel like.

"Ted was a dirty fighter," I continue. "He cut Donnie's eye with a bottle opener. Donnie jacked Ted upside his head, knocked him over the catwalk railing, and watched him fly through the air. Ted was shouting, 'I'll get you for this, you little sonofabitch.' When Ted fell into the molten steel, his skin bubbled like a boiled hot dog, and his glass eye popped right out of its socket. Every worker in the mill started clapping and cheering. Now Ted haunts old steel mills, looking for his glass eye. But he'll never find it, because Donnie shattered it with a hammer."

"I like that story," says Cornpup. "But you should've had Ted come back to life and claw Donnie's eyes out as revenge. That would've been more realistic."

"You should've told a story about a grain mill explosion," says Charlie. "Save the steel mill stories for when we're actually in a steel mill."

"Yeah, whatever," I mumble.

"Right here. I *told* you." Charlie stops in front of a hundred tall, blue metal barrels. He kicks a barrel with his boot, and the sound is not hollow. "It was real late, after midnight, probably, and I saw a really bright light, like those spotlights they have down at the salt barns, and some guys in hazmat suits were unloading barrels off a Mareno Chem flatbed."

"How'd they get in here?" says Cornpup. "The entrances are all boarded up."

"No," says Charlie. "Over by the loading docks, there are fresh chains on that door. I can't think of any other way."

He tosses me the flashlight and backs away from us. He is going to climb the grain elevator in the dark. He doesn't care if we watch him or not.

I stare down at the barrels. Could this really be it? It seems crazy that we'd find them so quickly. I can't find a label or a safety data sheet. And these babies are sealed tight.

"False alarm," says Cornpup.

I look at him.

"These barrels are aluminum. Phenzorbiflux could eat through aluminum in an hour."

"Then why the hazmat suits? Why go through all the trouble to dump these here in the middle of the night?"

"Mareno Chem dumps a lot of stuff in a lot of different places. I can't keep track of it all," says Cornpup. He looks at me with sad eyes. "I'm sorry, man. I know you were really hoping. But we'll keep looking. I'm with you on this."

Our barrel conversation is pierced by the sound of a metal structure breaking free of the ceiling. There are high-pitched squeals, like a million vampire bats. There is the deep industrial whine of ripping metal. So many sounds, so many echoes, and yet my ears are able to focus on one particular scream: Charlie.

CHAPTER 5
MISTAKES

MY veins are burning with adrenaline and fear. I close my eyes to get my bearings, to pretend this isn't happening. I don't even know where the grain elevator is.

"It wouldn't be by the loading docks," says Cornpup. "So let's go this way."

The interior of the mill is so much larger than it looks from the outside. We sprint, glass crunching under our shoes, flashlight slippery in my sweaty hand. I don't care if there are doors in the floor we can fall through. I'm not worried about slicing my leg on jagged machinery. I only care about finding Charlie.

"Don't die! We're coming!" Cornpup shouts.

Silence.

"Where are you?" I yell. "If you can hear me, say something!"

Silence.

I stop running. Cornpup bumps into me. The flashlight beam has snagged a fresh cloud of dust particles. A frightening heap of metal.

"That *was* a grain elevator," says Cornpup. He points toward a door near the ceiling. "It carried grain up there."

"I don't see any blood. That's good, right?" I begin picking up pieces of metal and tossing them away from the pile. "But what if he's buried?"

I don't see brains on the floor.

Together we lift heavy slabs of aluminum. The farther down we dig, the worse we feel. A pile like this could crush the top of a car, could turn human bones to splinters.

Something moves behind me. I whip around, and there is Charlie, covering his grin with his bandaged hand. "You guys were so worried. How *adorable*," he says.

Cornpup drops a huge metal pulley and stares at Charlie like he's trying to decide whether or not to punch him. "Are you nuts? What normal person wouldn't be worried?"

Charlie is doubled over with laughter.

"Don't speak to me," Cornpup says coldly. "Don't even come near me."

"What happened?" I can feel my heartbeat slowing to a more normal pace. "Were you on that thing when it fell?"

"Nope. I pulled on it to make sure it was secure, and it popped off the wall. When I screamed, it was funny. Don't lie."

"It wasn't funny." Cornpup's voice is a low growl.

Charlie grabs the flashlight out of my hand. "Anyway, the Mareno Chem trucks are parked over here. Come look."

It's true. There are seven white pickup trucks, each bearing the upbeat Mareno Chem logo—a green eagle sitting on planet Earth. Their logo has nothing to do with chemicals, and I think that's sort of the point.

Charlie takes Dad's switchblade from his pocket. It springs open. I remember how Dad used the blade to prune tomato plants.

"What's that for?" I ask him.

He stabs a tire, and it deflates quickly. The truck is now leaning forward and to the right. He stabs another tire and another.

"Don't," I say.

For Charlie, this is not about Mareno Chem or Phenzorbiflux or a fence around the creek. He just wants to destroy something, to hear the hiss of a ruined tire.

"Stop," I say.

Cornpup takes a can of spray paint from his paper bag. He shakes it, and I can hear the little metal ball bouncing around inside the canister. I look at him like he's nuts.

"They started it," he says. "They're the ones dumping chemicals illegally. This is me being nice. They deserve worse than spray paint."

He sprays STOP DUMPING HERE in red on one side of the nearest truck.

The fumes remind me to take off Dad's jacket. I turn it inside out and fold it into a neat square, which I then place on a ledge about ten feet away from Cornpup and the red spray paint.

"Here." Cornpup tosses me a canister of black. "Write something. It feels good."

I hesitate only a couple of seconds before shaking the can and spraying MONSTERS along one side of a truck. Along the other side I spray GET OUT OF HERE. Cornpup is right, this does feel good. We're sending a message to the people who took Dad away from me.

Cornpup writes, YOU COLOR OUR WATER, WE COLOR YOUR TRUCKS.

There is a burst of light.

We squint at the brightness.

A man yells, "What the hell is going on in here?"

Charlie says, "Oh crap."

We drop the paint cans and run.

I remember last summer, when Cornpup opened the Freak Museum in his bedroom. He started with a two-headed frog in a relish jar, and a huge, tumor-covered fish from Lake Erie in a jar that once held pickled eggs. Later he displayed a dead blue jay with deformed wings. Then I donated an old tennis shoe that melted when I stepped in a green puddle outside the dye facility. Charlie showed up with two dead squirrel babies, joined at the head. Almost once a week we would swim the creek with jars, until we had a whole collection of colored water samples that still shine like stained glass when you put a flashlight up to them. We were hunters, always looking for something strange and gory. When Cornpup found the corpse of a snake that exploded from trying to eat a mutant rat, Charlie said, "That's what I'd do if a snake tried to eat me. I'd bust right out of its stomach."

And that's what we do now—we bust out of the mill and run like animals. The adrenaline makes us faster.

"Do you think he saw us?" I say.

"No way," says Charlie.

When we pass the incinerator, we stop to rest.

Dad's jacket. I'm such an idiot.

"I left the jacket. I have to go back."

Charlie grabs my arm like he's gonna snap it. "Don't be stupid," he says. "That guy's not gonna find the jacket. He'll have enough to deal with when he sees what we did to those trucks. We can go back for the jacket later."

"When?"

"When things calm down," says Cornpup.

I don't speak the rest of the way home.

When we get back to Cardinal Drive, Mom is outside looking for me, which is not good.

I hear her desperately calling my name. Then I spot her standing under a streetlamp, fat rolls protruding from her stomach. She has outgrown her coat. She can't zip it. She holds it closed with her hands.

"Where were you?" She glares at Charlie, flashes a softer look at Cornpup.

"At my house," Cornpup says quickly.

She would faint in the middle of the street if she knew where we were. Her head would explode if we told her about the cat skeleton and the rat poison and the collapsed grain elevator and the unmarked barrels.

"You smell terrible," she says. "Jason, get in the house. You two, go home before I call your mothers."

Mom doesn't have the energy to punish me. She just gives me an irritated look and goes back to bed. I stay up for a while and watch TV in the den. I am very good at dozing off during the commercials and waking back up when the commercials are over, but at some point I accidentally stay asleep long enough to dream about a homeless guy frying salamanders over a tiny white fire.

"You're never going to find it," the man says to me. "Never, never, never."

I sit up. My mouth is dry. I think about my dream for a second. I try to decode the homeless guy's words. Never going to find Dad's jacket? Never going to find the missing Phenzorbiflux? Or maybe it's deeper than that—maybe I'm never going to find a path to revenge.

Probably the homeless guy meant nothing. Most dreams mean nothing.

CHAPTER 6
THREAT

KEVIN Thompson has two BB guns and a knife collection. I've seen him sit on his roof for hours, shooting birds out of the sky, laughing at piles of bloody feathers on the lawn. Last winter, he killed an owl right in front of us, and Charlie called him a psycho. When I think of Kevin, I think of robins getting picked off, one by one, like empty beer cans.

Today, when Kevin calls my house and says, "I'm gonna kill you for what you did at the grain mill," I hear little gunshots firing in the back of my mind.

Bang. Long pause. *Bang.* Long pause. *Bang, bang.*

"Did you hear me? I said I'm gonna *kill* you."

My heart is pounding so hard, I'm scared it will overheat like a radiator in July. I don't understand how some kid I barely know can all of a sudden hate me, *threaten my life*, over slashed tires and spray paint.

"Yeah, I heard you. But you've got the wrong guy. I've never even been to the mill."

Kevin laughs. "That was real stupid of you, leaving your old man's jacket by those trucks."

He knows I was there, and that changes things.

"Shouldn't you be out decapitating blue jays?" I say. "Or strangling hawks?" I breathe in slowly, trying to stay calm, when all I really want to do is break something.

"You won't get the jacket back," he says.

Bang. I close my eyes and see a seagull falling to the ground with a thud. *Bang.* I think about pigeons exploding. *Bang, bang.* Kevin will probably shred Dad's jacket with a hunting knife.

I slam the phone down, because I don't want to deal with this crap.

Outside our kitchen window, robins are swarming Mom's bird feeder. I feel like one of them now; I feel hunted. I think about what it will be like to start my freshman year with an enemy. I picture death threats in my locker, fights in the hall, raw eggs smacking against my front door.

My hands are shaking.

I get out my sketchbook and draw a mud demon roasting stray cats on a propane grill.

It's not fair that I'm taking all the heat for something that wasn't even my idea.

I press a blue pen to my skin and connect mosquito bites until I've drawn a choppy sea serpent tattoo on my forearm.

Charlie and Cornpup would've destroyed those trucks with or without me.

When the phone rings again, I answer it, but with a deeper

version of my own voice, like maybe I'm one of Dad's friends or the police.

It's Charlie.

"Why are you talking all weird?" he says.

I don't get into the whole Kevin Thompson thing, because there's still a chance this horrible situation could run its course, like chicken pox, without me having to do anything except sweat and drink lots of fluids.

Charlie says, "I thought up the best plan ever. Be at my house in five minutes. Cornpup's already here."

I change into a long-sleeved T-shirt and some cargo shorts. I'm hungry enough to eat a whole pizza, but instead I stuff a huge handful of potato chips into my mouth and run out the door.

The sky is dark steel, the color of machines. My dirt bike is out of gas, so I ride Dad's mountain bike to the end of our street. I hate the wind today; it smells like burning tires.

Charlie and Cornpup are eating beef jerky on the Pelliteros' front porch.

"Randy and Goat said we can hang with them," Charlie tells me. His right eye is purplish-red and swollen. His top lip is busted. "They're out past the mudflats."

"What happened to your face?" It's not a question I really need to ask. We all know Mr. Pellitero likes to give his sons an occasional knuckle sandwich. Charlie is amped up on adrenaline. He's talking so fast I have to really concentrate, and even then I don't hear the whole story.

". . . showed up at Mareno Chem drunk . . . on probation . . . face was all red when he got home . . . bottle of Jack Daniel's . . . wiped up the mess . . . glass everywhere . . . not my fault . . . didn't hurt . . . laughed in his face . . . Randy had to hold him back. . . ."

"Your dad should be in jail," Cornpup says in a bored voice.

"Oh yeah. That would be just great. Except let me tell you how it would really play out. He'd get fired from his job and my mom would use our savings to bail him out. Me and Randy already talked about it. We don't want him to be home all day, every day, hacking and coughing and drinking Jack on the couch in front of the TV. He needs to work and bring home a paycheck."

Charlie's right. We live in a blue-collar town. In this economy, you can't mess around. You work every day until the layoffs start. You work until your factory job doesn't exist anymore. If you're in with a good, strong company like Mareno Chem, you don't call in sick and you don't take vacation and you *definitely* don't get yourself thrown in jail. If Mr. Pellitero stops working, Randy will get kicked out of the house because he's over eighteen, and Charlie will have to play football with smashed-up pads and a cracked helmet. He can't risk disadvantages like that if he's gonna go pro.

"You're just delaying the inevitable," says Cornpup. "Going to jail is his *destiny*."

Charlie kicks the bag of beef jerky, and it flies all the way to the sidewalk. "Stop talking about him like that. Your family's not perfect. *People* aren't perfect."

Cornpup rolls his eyes. He doesn't know what it feels like when all the bills are suddenly paid by one parent instead of two, but I do. Me and Mom clip coupons and stalk garage sales. She trims her own hair over the sink. I bought myself a beat-up pair of snow boots at the Salvation Army. When our van blew a tire, we drove around on a donut for six months. At one point, she wanted to sell my new dirt bike, and I told her if she did, I'd leave and never come back.

I remember the first Christmas after Dad died. Our TV had sound but no picture. We didn't bother with a tree. For the first time since I was four years old, me and Dad would not be baking stollen together. I'd always hated that German fruitcake, with its strange ingredients: currants and almond extract, rum and orange peel, bright green candied cherries that looked like they'd been marinating in the colored waters of Two Mile Creek. But when Dad was gone, really gone, forever gone, I craved stollen all the time. There were no presents that year. Mom and I sat at the kitchen table and flipped through J. C. Penney catalogs. I pointed to things I thought she'd like and said, "I was going to buy you that for Christmas, but the store exploded right before I walked inside!" And she pointed to things she thought I'd like and said, "That's what I was going to buy you for Christmas, but some crazy lady with curlers in her hair stole the last one out of my cart!" We stayed up past midnight, playing this game, each excuse more ridiculous than the last, and it was actually pretty fun. I knew then that life would go on, that we would find a way to survive as a family. But it hasn't been easy. I don't think Cornpup could handle being as poor as us. He wants too many things.

We ride our bikes to the parking lot of what was once a steel ball company. Cornpup is balancing a huge duffel bag on his handlebars. Charlie is talking excitedly about the cookout tomorrow. He says there better be lots of ribs and wings. We pass the ruins of an old water treatment plant, weeds growing through the rubble, and I think how crazy it is that buildings die, just like people.

"I hate how the sky is always gray," Cornpup says. "It's never like this in Florida."

"You went there once. For, like, three days," I say.

"Three days of deep-sea fishing and girls in bikinis. My cousins live like gods."

"In a trailer park," says Charlie.

"I don't care. They swim in the ocean in *February*. I'd give up hockey for that. I'd give up anything for that."

"You should give up hockey anyway," says Charlie. "Because you suck."

Goat and Randy are sitting in the back of an abandoned pickup truck that has seen better days. All four tires are flat, the steering wheel is gone, and there's a thick layer of coal ash on the windshield. Randy moves empty beer cans out of the way so there's room for us to sit.

Goat says, "Oh great. The retards have arrived."

Randy tosses a pack of cigarettes to Charlie, who always has a book of matches in his pocket. "I don't think it's right that you can press a little button and get fire," Charlie once said to me. "Fire is not supposed to be automatic. You have to build it. You have to earn it."

Randy offers me a cold can of beer, and I take it. I lift the can to my lips, only pretending to drink, because it tastes horrible, like carbonated skunk juice.

"Me and Gina went to the Ashland site a couple nights ago." Goat has hundreds of tattoos, all interconnected. I wish my arms were covered like that. Permanent artwork on skin is so cool. "We were getting ready to set off some bottle rockets. Then five state agency trucks pulled up, and a bunch of guys started taking samples of the dirt and stuff."

"Intruders," says Charlie. "They're trying to take the creek away from us."

"The creek is poison," says Cornpup. "Just saying."

"Stop creating issues." Randy takes a long swig of beer. "We're here. We're alive."

Cornpup's got this stupid, smug look on his face. "You're alive *now*," he says. "But you're gonna get sick later. We all are."

Goat starts to laugh, and beer comes out of his nose. "I don't know, Cornpup. Seems to me you're the only reptile freak in this town. I don't have your webbed toes and shit."

"Leave him alone," says Charlie.

"Or what?"

"Or I'll bust your windshield with my crowbar some night when you're sleeping."

There is silence. Goat chewing on a toothpick. Charlie scraping paint from the truck bed. Randy balling his hands into fists. Finally Goat says, "You touch my car, and I'll kill you."

I laugh a little without meaning to. Goat could probably crush a metal barrel with his bare hands, but that's only because metal barrels can't run. Charlie is fast. Goat could never catch him, could never throw a punch that would actually hit him. Plus, Charlie isn't afraid to have puffed-up eyes or a broken jaw.

Lack of fear is the key.

Sometimes I wish I could be a Pellitero for a day. I wish I had their cocky faces, their cut-up muscles, their crazy peacock-blue eyes. At least Cornpup is here. Whatever happens, I will never be scrawnier than him. I will never have his ugly skin rashes or his owl eyes or his weird, webbed toes.

Randy changes the subject back to Goat's original story, about the unmarked trucks and stuff. "I can't believe you took Gina to the Ashland site," he says, laughing. "She must think you're a real romantic."

Goat scowls. "The Riverwalk's got cops all over the place. Can't shoot off fireworks there."

"Can't do other things there either," Randy says.

Goat slaps Randy a high five and says, "Exactly."

Charlie knows what they're talking about, and so do I. We saw Randy kissing a girl out by the creek once, and not small kisses either. It was like he was going to swallow her face. And we saw a pink bra by the water.

Cornpup knows nothing about girls. When he's around Randy and Goat, he's always lost, looking to me and Charlie for clues. "What's a hickey?" he once asked me.

I told him it looked sort of like a bruise.

Then he asked me if I wanted to give Valerie a hickey, and I told him to piss off.

"My dad's taking me and Randy out to Erie on Saturday," says Charlie. "We're gonna fish for pike. Maybe some tumor heads if we're lucky."

"I'm coming with you," says Cornpup.

"No you're not," says Randy.

"I'll stay out of the way. I just need to get some seagull skeletons for the Freak Museum."

"You can't just invite yourself," says Charlie.

The first time I saw a tumor head, I was ten years old. I held the fat fish in my hands, staring, horrified, at the golf ball–sized growths all over its body. One of the tumors leaked yellow fluid onto my fingers. I tried scrubbing my skin with lake water and sand, but the stench stayed with me for days.

"This time of year the seagull eggs are all hatching," says Randy.

"I hate seagulls." Goat spits phlegm into an empty beer can. "They're taking over the world. You should crush a few hundred eggs with your hockey stick. Do us all a favor."

"Speaking of favor," says Charlie. "We need you to get us into the Mareno Chem building."

"No," says Goat. "No way. That's what you little retards came out here to ask me? My old man was out of work for seven months. Now he's finally working, and you think I'm gonna put his job on the line for you? Get out of here."

I hate Goat. Everyone hates Goat. I have no idea why Randy is friends with him. It makes no sense.

"Just steal his keys for one hour," says Charlie.

"No. I said no."

"Come on."

There's a loud metallic boom in the distance. Maybe a shipping crane dropped something. Or maybe a machine exploded.

Goat smirks at Charlie. "I heard Mareno Chem is closing building A. That's bad news for you. The way your old man drinks, he ain't gonna find a new job around here."

"It's not closing." Charlie speaks too quickly, which tells me the rumor might be true.

"They've been giving him overtime," Randy adds. "I don't see how they can shut the whole mill down if there's so much work."

Goat looks at me, hard. "Because some people thought it would be cute to screw up the Phenzorbiflux project. Now Mareno Chem keeps moving jobs to their Dayton branch."

So Goat is another one who thinks Dad intentionally caused the accident. It never ends. I'm so sick of people blaming our family for the pay cuts and the layoffs. Yeah, Dad thought Phenzorbiflux was too unpredictable and dangerous. Yeah, he told everyone production should slow down, maybe even stop. That doesn't mean he released the toxic soup on purpose. The safety latches must've failed. The gauges must've malfunctioned.

I scratch a mosquito bite on my leg until it bleeds.

"We have to get into that building. It's real important," says Charlie.

It turns out that the night I lost Dad's jacket, Charlie ran back to the grain mill, alone, at two in the morning. His plan was to slip in and out of the building, quick and quiet, like a spy. All he had to do was rescue the jacket and run. Illegal dumpers don't call the cops, so it was gonna be Charlie up against one security guard, which is almost no contest at all.

Except there was a silver Lexus in the parking lot.

Charlie saw three men arguing. He knew all their faces.

The mayor's deputy was shouting, "Vandals destroyed seven

trucks on your shift! *Seven trucks!* Do you know what that means? It means you're finished here."

Jack Thompson, the security guard who came so close to catching us at the mill, said, "Please. I'll do anything. I really need this job."

The Mareno Chem executive with the silver Lexus balled up Dad's jacket and whipped it into his backseat. "I'll find out who this belongs to. And we'll make sure this little problem goes away."

That's when Charlie took off running.

We all have questions.

Goat says, "Are you talking about the jacket with the drum set on the back? *That* jacket! You wore it to the mill? You *left it* there?"

Cornpup says, "So let me get this straight. The mayor's deputy knows about the dumping?"

Randy says, "They're gonna trace that jacket back to Jason so quick, it's not even funny. What were you idiots thinking?"

I feel my throat dry up like I just swallowed a handful of dirt. "The security guard who got fired . . . is he Kevin Thompson's dad?"

No wonder he wants to kill me. *Bang.* I shut my eyes and imagine a dead swan floating in the creek.

Charlie says, "I was wondering when you were gonna figure that out."

Goat is quiet for a long time. "Okay. I'll let Jason into the building for fifteen minutes."

Charlie wants to know why we can't all go in. Goat tells him it's because the three of us are a disaster waiting to happen.

Charlie blows smoke in Goat's face. "Fine. When?"

"Monday night at nine," Goat says to me. "If you're a minute late, I'm gone."

The pressure is officially on. I want the jacket back, yes, but I don't want to go into the Mareno Chem building alone, after hours, after what we did.

Cornpup grabs his duffel bag and stands. The truck bed bounces at the shift in weight. "I have to go," he says. "I have to get to the pawnshop before it closes."

"What've you got in there?" Randy asks.

"None of your business," says Cornpup.

I think Charlie wants to stay. So do I. Randy has been so moody and distant lately. He's always out drag racing with Goat. Or he's playing his guitar with his bedroom door locked. Or he's at some girl's house. When we finally get a chance to hang with him, it's hard to walk away.

I climb onto my bike and hear Goat say, "Wearing a dead man's custom leather jacket to the industrial yards. Unbelievable."

I look back, expecting to see a smile on Randy's face, expecting them both to be mocking us as we pedal off. Instead, I see Randy shove Goat hard against the cab of the truck. "Why do you always have to be such an asshole?" he says.

I wonder if it's possible that Randy will someday dump his dead-beat friend, drop the attitude, and come back to us.

CHAPTER 7
TWO MILE CREEK

WE follow an access road until it dead-ends. We cut through a dried-up pond. We pass a baseball diamond that has all its benches and bleachers ripped up. Our town has one main drag, with a hair salon, a pool hall, a liquor store, and two family restaurants. There's also a pretty cool pawnshop, which is where we're headed now.

"You're such a hustler," Charlie says to Cornpup. "Always selling something."

Today the pawnshop guy takes one look at Cornpup's duffel bag and rolls his eyes. "I'm closing in two minutes."

There are so many things I want in this store—a Fender guitar, speakers and amps, a rotisserie oven, a blue lava lamp, and a watch that tells you what time it is in four different countries.

"I brought some good stuff this time," Cornpup says. "Check it out."

Pawnshop Guy squints through his glasses. "I'll give you a couple bucks for these cell phones. I'll buy the tools off you too. But that's it. I don't want that space heater. I've got plenty of space heaters."

"Fine. Whatever," says Cornpup. "Can I use your bathroom?"

"As long as you're quick about it. I have to be at the bowling alley in twenty minutes." Pawnshop Guy is eating slices of bologna straight from the package without any bread.

Dad used to bowl in a league. His bowling ball was black with swirls of green, like a giant marble. The night he died, Mom sat in a kitchen chair with that ball on her lap for hours, until I told her to stop it because she was scaring me.

"Hey." Pawnshop Guy frowns at us. "Where does your weird little friend get all these electronics? Is he a thief? Tell me the truth."

"He knows how to fix other people's junk," says Charlie. "He's like a half-insane engineer."

"I feel like I hemorrhage money to that boy. What does he do with it all?"

"Donates it to a museum." I'm not lying. Cornpup dumps a lot of cash into our Freak Museum—colored lights, labels for each exhibit, formaldehyde, and hardware for the growing shelves. It gets expensive.

Pawnshop Guy says, "Museum, my ass."

Cornpup appears two seconds later with a wet piece of paper in his hands. "I just found this in the garbage. The Army Corps of Engineers is hosting a meeting about Two Mile Creek next week. Contamination. Anybody from the neighborhood can go. You know what that means?"

"It means we'll have to jump a stupid fence every time we want to go swimming next summer," Charlie says in a bored voice.

"I already know about the meeting," I tell them. "My mom got a letter in the mail."

Pawnshop Guy gives Cornpup a small wad of cash. Then we head outside.

Cornpup has a serious look on his face. "They're taking public comments. We can tell them about Phenzorbiflux."

"Comments are weak," says Charlie. "If you want to bring down the biggest chemical company in the world, it's gonna take more than *comments*."

I have to agree. "Plus, they use psychological warfare. Every time someone speaks out against them, they lay off a bunch of people and threaten to shut down the Poxton plant. Then the whole town turns on you. Bring up Phenzorbiflux and twenty-five jobs disappear, guaranteed."

"They make everyone feel afraid," says Cornpup. "That's their one power over us. But what if we refuse to feel the fear? Then they're powerless."

"It's not fear," says Charlie. "It's using your head. It's survival. You don't work at Mareno Chem. And your parents don't work at Mareno Chem. Some of us need those paychecks."

"Then why do we keep looking for the barrels?" says Cornpup. "What's the point of finding Phenzorbiflux if we can't tell anyone?"

"The point," I tell him, "is to find the Phenzorbiflux before *you* open your big mouth. If we stir up trouble now, and people lose their jobs, and we've got no proof to back us up, then what? Then we've blown our big chance. If you talk at this meeting, you gotta promise me you'll focus on the smaller chemical companies who've been dumping in the creek. Don't bring up Mareno Chem at all."

Cornpup considers this, but he won't look at me, and I can tell he's pissed.

Charlie says, "Here's the deal. We'll keep looking for the missing Phenzorbiflux, because it's fun. And we'll go to this stupid meeting, because we can't trust Cornpup to keep his mouth shut otherwise.

But when it comes time to really punish Mareno Chem, we're gonna do something big. No more talk."

I feel a surge of adrenaline. I wish I knew what Charlie had in mind.

Cornpup is in a pissy mood now. He trudges behind us, whining about how we shouldn't go to the creek today because the smell is too strong.

"He can go sweat to death, for all I care," says Charlie. "It's crazy hot out. I'm going swimming."

It's not like we don't get it, about the creek being gross and dangerous or whatever. We know bubbling gray water with marble swirls of black sludge ain't exactly pure, but New York City is a major terrorist target, and nobody moves away on account of that. Hell, there were people who wouldn't even *temporarily* leave New Orleans when Katrina was a couple of miles offshore.

We've got our home, a place that's ours, things we love doing, and we just roll with it. Charlie says it's really unhealthy to live in constant fear. He says you can live forever if you laugh and take a lot of risks.

On the way to the industrial yards, we pass Kevin Thompson's house. His garage is open and his bike is gone, but I still glance up at his roof to see if he's perched there with his guns.

"I'm just so pissed off," I say. "It's not even my fault he wants to kill me. If his dad was a great security guard, they wouldn't've fired him for what we did at the grain mill. He was probably already on thin ice for something else."

"Yeah, the two of you are gonna be enemies for a while." Charlie swipes a football from someone's front lawn. He jogs back to us with a huge smile on his face. "I heard he wants to hook up with Valerie, so if you go out with her, it's like a double whammy. You think he hates you now, just wait."

48

"I'm lifting weights in your garage tonight," I say. "When he kills me, I want my gravestone to say I fought back."

At the creek, me and Charlie toss the football around while Cornpup digs for the eternal robot. We call it that because he never stops tweaking it, giving it little remote-controlled weapons, lengthening its legs, outfitting it with cool armor. He pulls the robot up out of the earth. He peels off the blue tarp covering and then checks to make sure no dirt got into the controls. Minutes later, the robot is walking through water, firing Nerf rockets at my head. Charlie finds our Super Soakers in one of the other tunnels. He tosses me one, and then it's like there's this all out battle, me and Charlie against Cornpup's machine. We're in the water, drenched, our shorts pretty much falling down, and Cornpup's onshore, bone-dry, punching commands into his controller, with this crazy look on his face, shouting, "You guys are dead!"

So me and Charlie have no choice but to make balls of creek mud and start whipping them at Cornpup's face. It's really the most kick-ass battle we've ever had. By the end, me and Charlie are all slimy and green from the water, and Cornpup is covered in mud, and our faces are burning from laughing so hard. When it starts getting dark, we split up. Cornpup stays at the creek to rebury the eternal robot. Charlie is starving and runs home to eat. I feel so grimy, I can't even think about food. All I want to do is take a shower.

Before I go into my house, I strip off most of my clothes and abandon them in a garbage can by the street. I wring out my sneakers, dripping green water onto our porch steps. I wipe my feet clean in the grass. A long, hot shower turns out to be the perfect thing. I change into jeans and a black T-shirt. Then I call Cornpup.

"You don't have to actually *lift* anything," I promise him. "We aren't gonna force you to work out. Just come hang with us."

He tells me he got creek water in his eyes. He doesn't feel so great. He's going to bed.

So it ends up being just me and Charlie lifting weights in the Pelliteros' garage. We have the radio cranked up. We're mocking Cornpup, who's probably all curled up in bed right now like a granny.

"Oh, Mommy, my eyes are stinging; make me some soup," says Charlie.

"Oh, Mommy, I pooped the bed and it smells like ammonia," I say.

"Oh, Mommy, help me get all this toxic mud out of my ears," says Charlie.

Valerie and Jill show up out of nowhere, and I start freaking out in my head, because what if Val heard me say "pooped the bed" and doesn't know I was pretending to be Cornpup?

I turn down Charlie's metal music.

"You guys going to the cookout tomorrow?" Jill asks us.

Charlie drops his dumbbells. His arm muscles look ripped. "Hell yeah, we're going."

Valerie is sitting on a weight bench, legs crossed, staring at her hands. She looks up at me once, and I swear she likes it that I'm all sweaty with bloodshot eyes. Maybe I look dangerous.

We talk about dumb stuff for about ten minutes. Then Charlie gets restless because he wants to start lifting again, and the girls say they have to get going because they were supposed to be walking to the video store and straight back, and Jill's parents will kill them if they find out about this little detour. Valerie hands me a folded-up piece of pink paper, and I shove it into my pocket to read later, when Charlie's not around. Then the metal music is back on, and the girls take off.

I do push-ups till my arms give out. I do crunches till it hurts to breathe. Charlie doesn't get tired. He only stops because he can see I'm cashed.

We go inside to make some food, but when we enter the kitchen, there is trouble. Mr. Pellitero is drunk, staggering near the sink. Mrs. Pellitero is shouting in his face, "What are we going to do for money?" over and over again.

Randy says, "Mom, calm *down*. There are other jobs. We'll be fine."

Mrs. Pellitero says, "No, Randy, we aren't gonna be fine. All the good jobs are getting shipped off to China, and your father thinks he can just screw around. Moving to another town won't do no good. Jobs have been disappearing all over the country."

Charlie jumps right in on the argument, veins bulging from his arms. "Mareno Chem fired you? For what? What did you do?" he shouts in his dad's face.

Mrs. Pellitero is making the situation so much worse. She keeps saying, "Now what are we gonna do? Now what are we gonna do? Now what are we gonna do?"

I know something bad is about to happen when I see the empty bottle of Jäger on the floor. Mr. Pellitero pops his wife in the eye with one quick, precise punch that makes me want to spit in his face. Then Charlie gives me the look, *Jason, go home*, and I take off running.

CHAPTER 8
COOKOUT

MOM is the only person I know who'd spend an entire morning talking about Polish sausage. "It's hot out today," she says. "And this meat was expensive. I'm not taking any chances." She sends me to the basement in search of a cooler.

"The Kuperskis live across the street. Why can't we just use a plastic bag full of ice?"

"Go find the cooler, Jason. Now."

Our basement is such a mess. I step over lawn chairs, oil cans, a baseball bat and cleats. I move gardening tools, dead tomato plants, a broken fan, and a bag of topsoil. Things we couldn't sell in our yard sale. A deflated soccer ball. A dented drum set. Broken furniture we'll never fix or use. Why am I the one who has to dig through all this junk?

I woke up hungry. Today is the Kuperskis' annual cookout, and they put out a huge spread, lots of meats and hot dishes. They don't just invite people from Cardinal Drive either; they invite the whole neighborhood. Sid Kuperski is friends with a man who brings piles of hot wings packed in aluminum catering pans. Gloria Kuperski makes a mean six-layer taco dip, which is my all-time favorite food. Charlie doesn't have a favorite food. He'll eat anything, especially if there's red meat or chocolate involved. The only person I know who doesn't live for the Kuperskis' cookout is Cornpup, because nothing grosses him out more than food from other people's houses. He thinks there's going to be a hair ball baked into one of the garlic meatballs, boogers in the pretzel cake, and weird strains of salmonella growing in the potato salad. He says there's no end to the terrible things that can go on in a kitchen that's not regulated by the FDA. If he comes to a cookout at all, he'll bring his own grilled cheese sandwiches in a paper bag. But usually he doesn't come.

"The cooler isn't down here," I shout. My tone is whiny, but I don't really care. I'm not in the greatest of moods. I got about a hundred prank calls last night. I had to stay awake watching a horror movie marathon, picking up each call midway through the first ring. Otherwise our kitchen phone would wake up Mom. I try to think of something creepier than Kevin Thompson calling my house, again and again, never saying anything, heavy metal blasting in the background, but that's about as creepy as it gets.

The cooler is under Dad's camping equipment.

At first, I just stare. I am ambushed by a memory. It was two summers ago. I was at the beach with Mom, who was skinny then, and Dad, who would not live through the winter. I raced Dad to the pier, and I won. Seagulls were everywhere. Mom had filled the cooler with bologna sandwiches and cans of pop. She kept saying she was gonna "get a tan, dammit," and Dad told her not to use vegetable oil, because he didn't want to her turning into a lobster. I waded in the water, but it was kind of cold. It was going to be a good day, a family day, and I felt luckier than Charlie then, because my dad would never snap his belt at me, would never pass out drunk on the couch with a lit cigarette.

But the day got cut short. A sudden storm rolled up on Lake Erie. The entire sky turned the color of dirty aluminum. A cold, hard rain began to fall. Mom picked up the blanket, and we all started running. Dad had the cooler. I had Mom's beach chair. We were all giggling. We took Highway 5 home, past Bethlehem Steel and the Coast Guard base, over the Skyway bridge. Mom turned the radio up and sang in her bluesy voice. I can't remember what the song was, and it bothers me that I can't remember.

Dad was the last person to carry this cooler. I don't want to touch it. I don't want to be the one to wipe his fingerprints away.

"It's about time," Mom says to me. "I thought you got lost down there." She makes me take the cooler out back and rinse it with the hose. Then she makes me put a T-shirt on. "You're not going to the Kuperskis' in swim trunks. You'll look like a hillbilly." Never mind how she's wearing puffy Windbreaker shorts and a MERV'S HOT DOGS T-shirt big enough to be a pop-up tent.

I walk to the back porch and turn on the hose. I rinse dried grass and a suspicious gooey pink stain from inside the cooler. I flood a couple of anthills, just because I can. I am pretty much in a daze. Dad is on my mind, no matter how hard I try to push the thoughts away. I could stand here forever, just letting the water run and run and run.

"Jason! How long does it take to rinse out a cooler?" Mom says. "Charlie's on the phone."

I turn off the faucet. I'm supposed to coil the hose over a hook on the side of our house, but that'll take too long. As a rule, Charlie doesn't hold on the line for more than a minute or two, if that. I leave the hose in a sloppy heap and jog back to the house.

"Holy loudness. What's going on over there?" Charlie asks. He's eating something crunchy.

"My aunt Ellen just pulled up in her crappy car. You're supposed to be on your way over here. Is Cornpup with you?"

"He's sick again."

"Oh. Did you get the candy?"

"Nope. Randy wouldn't take me to the store. But we have Popsicles in the freezer."

"Those'll be good," I say. "But hurry up. My mom's making me do stupid little jobs around the house."

Charlie hangs up without saying goodbye.

Mom says, "Do you want to tell me who kept calling at all hours last night? Was that Charlie?"

"No," I say. "Some little kids found our number in the phone book, is all."

Ellen, who is skinny, walks into our house without knocking. She's carrying a casserole dish in one hand, and my little cousin, Bryan, on her hip. She says, "Lynn, you're going to be hot in that big old T-shirt," and I shoot her a dirty look, because I don't care if it's nine thousand degrees outside; Mom should be wearing more clothing, not less.

"Wow, so you're going to be a high schooler in a couple of months," Ellen says to me. "Are you excited?"

"Not really," I say, but she's only half listening.

Mom runs into the bathroom to change. She comes out wearing a one-piece bathing suit and the same pair of Windbreaker shorts, but *without* a shirt. She embarrasses me constantly. I don't get a break.

When Dad died, Mom started eating double helpings of everything; sometimes she even goes back for thirds. I don't think she all of a sudden got hungrier. I just think the sadness dug a real deep hole in her, and she's trying to fill it with stuff that tastes good. Things haven't been easy for her, I know, but she's not the only one hurting. And it's not like it would be that hard for her to ride her bike to the air products plant a few times a week. Or eat salads every once in a while.

I go to my room and find a T-shirt to wear with my swim trunks. When I return to the kitchen, Bryan is holding a bag of balloons.

"Fill these with water for me," he says. He is standing on a step stool and has already tried to fill two blue balloons himself, but they've exploded in the sink.

"Fill them yourself," I say. Ellen goes out back to smoke a cigarette.

"Hey, guys." Charlie has let himself in. He doesn't look angry or embarrassed. It's like the things I saw last night—the bottle of Jäger, the crying mom, a fist to the eye—never happened. He tosses a box of Popsicles into the freezer. He has on an old Sabres ball cap with tar on the brim. He drinks our green Kool-Aid straight from the pitcher.

"Charlie! Charlie!" Bryan shouts. "Fill these for me, okay?"

Charlie is always nice to little kids, which is something I've never understood. He fills thirty water balloons to a near-bursting size, while Bryan jumps in place for a full minute, the way he does when someone flushes a toilet and he gets to see the water swirl.

I help Charlie pile the water balloons into a laundry basket. He gives Bryan a Popsicle, and Mom makes him eat it on the front porch, because she just mopped the floor. I'm so hungry I can't make it to the porch; I eat my Popsicle over the sink.

Ellen comes in from outside and almost drops the potted plant she's carrying. "Charlie, my God! You're so tall. You and Randy could be twins!"

"I'll be way stronger than Randy by the end of summer," says Charlie.

Mom packs suntan oil and a hairbrush into her purse. She tells Charlie to stop drinking all our Kool-Aid. Then she says, "Your mom's not coming? Is she busy with her flowers?"

I glare at her. She already knows Mrs. Pellitero has a black eye. I told her what happened last night, because I had to tell someone, and she promised not to say anything.

Charlie looks down at his sneakers. "She's not feeling well."

"Did she send a dish along with you?"

"He brought Popsicles," I say quickly.

Charlie's hand covers his mouth as he grins. Either he doesn't pick up on Mom's nastiness or he doesn't care. He gets the box out of the freezer. "Want one, Mrs. Hammond? I got grape, cherry, or green."

I almost laugh out loud. She never says no to food these days.

She chooses grape. "Didn't Randy apply for a warehouse job at Mareno Chem a while back?"

"Yeah," says Charlie. "They never called him, though. It's hard to get a job there because the pay's so good. There's a wait list or whatever."

"Interesting," says Mom. "Because I heard someone shot and killed a whole bunch of birds and then piled the corpses in front of the Mareno Chem administrative office. Did your brother have something to do with that?"

Charlie stops smiling. "Randy wouldn't shoot birds."

"So that's your story and you're sticking with it, eh?"

"What's that supposed to mean?" I glare at Mom.

Charlie is as quiet as a stone.

We make our way out the door, single file. Charlie carries the cooler. Mom has her beach bag. I lug the basket of balloons. Bryan follows us across the street, shooting our backs with his squirt gun. I think of Kevin Thompson, how he probably would shoot me in the back with real bullets if he could get away with it.

"What a beautiful day," Mom says. "Blue skies still feel so new to me. When I was growing up, back when the steel industry was really booming, ore dust and ash from the Bethlehem Steel furnaces used to block the sun, making the sky glow orange, like it was the end of the world, like the waterfront was on fire. It's so different now. Buffalo gets a lot of sunshine, and over here, we've got smoggy skies mostly."

I know what she means. Whenever we drive along the shores of Lake Erie, it's like touring a ruined kingdom. You see castle-sized factories; rotting barges with no freight on board; giant smokestacks, like organ pipes, cutting through the sky; and you realize it's all a bunch of skeletons. Industry is dead in Buffalo. The warehouses and foundries still in operation are found here, in Poxton. You look out your window most days and you see swirling gray till you're almost seasick. Sometimes we get a different kind of smoke, opaque white in color, and my sinuses drip down the back of my throat, filling my mouth with a weird taste that makes me think of rubber bands.

Today is a great day, though. Today I don't catch a whiff of anything I don't like. Burgers, a charcoal grill, citronella candles, and fireworks. That's how summer should always smell.

The Kuperskis' backyard is filled with people. Sid has on a plastic apron. He's got a split-level grill with wings on the top, hot dogs on the bottom. Gloria, dressed in red, serves drinks. Every glass is topped off with a paper umbrella.

Valerie and Jill are at the far end of the yard, sunbathing on lawn chairs. "Two hot girls and free food," says Charlie. "This cookout officially rules."

I stand next to him, frozen. Sometimes I wonder why Charlie, who always takes the best of everything, has chosen Jill—a cute girl, yes, but not *gorgeous*. Val is the really pretty one. I can't believe I forgot to read her note last night. It's still folded up in my jeans at home.

"Why are they giggling?" I ask Charlie.

"Girls giggle. That's what they *do*."

All summer, I've been waiting for this day. I came here to stuff my face and get barbecue sauce all over my T-shirt and do cannonballs into the pool and have a food fight with Charlie. Now my appetite is sort of gone.

Valerie is smiling at us, or maybe at me, and I pretend not to notice her. I'm not like Charlie, who can stand over a pile of greasy wings and still look cool. Charlie, who isn't shaken up by suntan oil and bikini straps.

"That bikini is . . . Wow," I say.

Mom sits at a card table with some of her friends from the air products plant. Two of the women have already been in the pool; their hair is stringy and wet. Ellen flirts with a mechanic, some guy with biceps the size of car batteries, while Bryan digs holes in the pile of fly ash that spilled over the privacy fence. Three men I don't recognize are drinking beer on the Kuperskis' roof. One of them jumps into the shallow pool, and I am sure he's going to snap his neck and die, but he climbs out of the water with a triumphant grin on his face, and a couple people laugh and cheer like he's some kind of hero.

Risky behavior. Dad would never have done that, and he's dead, while this jumping-off-the-roof guy is alive and *happy*. It's like a bad math problem. I don't get it. I really don't.

Charlie bites his thumbnail. "I might out-eat your mom today. There's a very good chance."

"Not even possible. She's been sucking down cookies since we got here. She has an insurmountable lead."

I'm not a horrible person. I don't exactly like it that we rip on

59

Mom all the time, but if she wouldn't eat so much, people wouldn't say stuff.

"What's up with that guy who keeps jumping off the roof?" says Charlie. "He's splashing all the water out of the pool."

"We should tell him to stop. Sid won't say anything. He's too nice."

"Or we could just swim at Two Mile later." For Charlie, our creek is always the first, best choice.

The Jell-O salads are attracting flies. One card table, the one filled with brownies and Polish desserts, is surrounded by kids. We carry our plates to an unoccupied table next to a picnic bench, where Theresa Seaver is fanning herself with a Frisbee. Theresa was one of the people who told Dad to keep his mouth shut when Mareno Chem resumed production of Phenzorbiflux. She told him it was a secret project so he should mind his own business. He said five-ton containers of an illegal chemical *was* his business, especially when he was forced to work with it every day in the processing plant. She was supposed to be his friend, but she couldn't risk losing her job. And when he died, she still didn't speak up about Phenzorbiflux. She just shrugged her shoulders, like Dad was crazy.

I wolf down a burger, some chips and salsa, and a piece of pie. Charlie flings chunks of potato salad at me, because he knows I hate the smell of mayonnaise. Peggy, Mom's line manager at the air products plant, sits down next to Theresa. They start talking about the newest rumor: Mareno Chem is developing a new product line. Pesticides. That could mean more jobs here in Poxton. Or more jobs at their Ohio facility. No one knows for sure yet.

That sounds about right. Mareno Chem took everything from me. But they keep growing, making money. Nobody cares.

Near the pool, Bryan is crying. Ellen is kneeling beside him. He shows her his elbow. I want to go talk to Valerie, but first I have to think of something good to say.

Charlie bites into a sausage. Grease spills down the front of his shirt. "Guess what's happening one week from now?"

I make a face. "Hmmm. Let's see. I have to get through Monday night without Goat locking me in the Mareno Chem building. And Kevin the bird slayer is now stalking me, so one week from now I'll probably be facedown in the dirt and you'll be picking BBs out of the back of my head with tweezers."

Charlie laughs.

And then, like I summoned him or something, Kevin Thompson rolls up on his dirt bike.

CHAPTER 9
BUZZ KILL

"UN-EFFING-BELIEVABLE," I say as I watch Kevin and his friend Damon skip the food and make a beeline to the sunbathers.

Charlie shakes his head at me. "Val is gonna try to make you jealous. You have to play it like you don't even notice."

"I can't stand this. I want to go over there."

"That would be stupid," says Charlie. "Trust me on this."

Play it cool. I interpret that to mean, *Don't look over at Val no matter what.* That's about as cool as I can get.

"So like I was saying." Charlie takes another bite of sausage. "The neighborhood meeting about Two Mile is a week from today. Cornpup is hell-bent on talking. We're gonna have to go to this thing and keep an eye on him."

"I'd rather stab my eyes out with a hot poker. But you're right. He's such a big mouth."

Mom's line manager looks over at us. "I couldn't help but over-hear. Are you talking about that meeting they're having about all the chemicals in the creek and whatnot?"

"Leave them alone, Peggy. They're eating." Theresa has a deep laugh, a smoker's laugh.

Peggy makes a face. "The creek is a mess. That's the honest-to-God truth. It can't hurt to have someone clean it up."

"They're not gonna *clean it up*," says Charlie. "They're gonna fence it off."

Theresa snorts. "Don't tell my girls that. They swim in that creek all summer long. A fence is just about the worst thing you could do to them."

Peggy folds and unfolds her hands. She is a hard-core factory worker: no painted nails, no rings on her fingers, just calluses and scars. She says, "As much as I hate to think it, I feel like there's something real bad in that creek. I just get a terrible feeling in my stomach."

"Subject change," says Theresa. "Jason, honey. How are you doing? How's your mom doing?" This is one of those questions that sound as light as air, except I know better. She really means to ask, *How are you doing? How's your mom doing? Because your dad is* dead *now, so you can't be doing too well.*

I look down at my burger.

"Rich was, wow, just a wonderful man, a good friend. I sure do miss him."

"You're part of the reason he's gone," I say in a cold voice.

Theresa looks genuinely confused. "What do you mean, honey?"

I focus my eyes on a fly that's buzzing around Charlie's plate. Anger is churning inside me, gathering momentum like some horrible, unmanned machine. I want to throw my plate at Peggy's face. I want to smear potato salad in Theresa's hair.

"Don't get him started on this," Charlie says. "He doesn't want to talk about this."

Peggy places a rough hand on my shoulder. "I think I know why you're upset. Your dad believed they were forcing him to process Phenzorbiflux under another name. He believed they were tampering with his safety gear. But it just wasn't true."

"Stop it." My hand slams down on the card table. Charlie's soda spills everywhere. "Just stop talking."

A panicked expression washes over Peggy's face. "I'm sorry. I just wanted you to know that we don't blame him. We know he was just confused. . . ."

Tears burn my eyes. Dad knew how to build bookshelves. He made minestrone soup from scratch. He was a drummer. He grew tomatoes in our backyard. He saved an injured hawk once. He wanted to take my mom to Vegas. And he liked watching shows about sharks. He had a football signed by the entire Bills team. He had a Minotaur tattooed on his right shoulder blade. He wasn't *confused*. I will not let people talk about him over soggy paper plates and baked beans. I will stand up and scream if they don't shut their pieholes.

"I'm out of here." I storm out of the Kuperskis' backyard, not caring if Valerie is watching, and not worrying about Kevin and his guns. I don't stop until I reach the middle of our street, which right now feels like a safe zone.

Charlie is right behind me.

"Go away." The last thing I need is for Charlie to see me cry.

"Jason, they're idiots. Your dad wouldn't want you missing this cookout because of them. He'd want me to drag you back to the table so you can see what I'm about to do."

The tone of Charlie's voice surprises me. No cockiness, no

sarcasm. He knows there's a tear falling down my cheek, and he doesn't even care. I wipe my nose with my thumb.

"What are you about to do?" I feel an unexpected smile forming at the corners of my mouth.

Charlie runs back to the cookout. I follow him. A really old Springsteen song blasts from a speaker on the deck. Adults are buzzed. Little kids are playing. Charlie grabs two water balloons from Bryan's basket and whips one of them at me with his pitching arm. The water balloon hits me hard in the chest. My T-shirt is drenched.

So he wants to have a water balloon fight? No problem.

I run to the basket and grab some balloons to throw back at him. I also grab Bryan's squirt gun and tuck it into the back of my swim trunks. I don't have a strong throwing arm, but I'll wait until that one perfect second, when Charlie gets distracted. I'll launch my balloons at close range, pelting him so hard he'll have red marks on his back.

I hear shrieking. Commotion. I turn around.

There are pieces of a busted pink balloon in Theresa's hair. Her white tank top is soaked. You can totally see her bra. Peggy's chunky eye makeup is running down her face like motor oil.

"You little scumbag!" she shouts at Charlie. "What is your problem?"

Charlie shrugs. "Sorry, lady. I guess my hand slipped."

But he is a precision pitcher. A quarterback. When he throws something, he hits his target. He doesn't slip. Ever.

The Kuperskis shake their heads. The way people glare at Charlie, it makes me feel like I got punched in the stomach. Even Mom, with a cookie in her hand, is scowling. Val and Jill stare at us, wide-eyed. Kevin and Damon are smirking. I know what they're all thinking: *Of course he ruined the party. A bad seed from a bad family; it's to be expected.* But all these good people from good families, they turned their backs on Dad when he needed them most. They chose factory jobs over a dear friend. Charlie would never sell out like that.

"Look at them," he says. "The same people who are all mad right now are gonna be cheering for me when I'm playing linebacker this fall. That's the thing with a mob mentality. These people get happy together, and they get mad together, and if you pull one person out of the crowd, that person won't know what the hell is going on."

Gloria brings Peggy and Theresa a towel.

It's crazy how a small taste of revenge makes me feel so happy. It's like the whole crying thing never happened. If I could just somehow punish Mareno Chem for what they did to us, I bet I'd never feel depressed ever again.

When we leave the cookout, Val and Jill look crushed. I think they expected us to go over and talk to them, but we don't have to do what they expect. Out of the corner of my eye I see Kevin watching me so close it's like he's peering through the scope of a sniper's rifle, but I don't even care. We stop at Cornpup's house and throw loose pieces of asphalt at his window, and when he doesn't look out at us from behind his plastic blinds, we just laugh and say he must still be pooping the bed. Then Goat drives by with Randy and two girls in his car. He flips us off, and Randy laughs.

"What was that all about?" I say.

"Who knows."

Before walking up his driveway, Charlie stops and does something I've never seen him do before. He picks litter up off the street. A crushed soda can, a Snickers wrapper, an empty pack of Camels. Without uttering a single word, he tosses it all into his garbage can and closes the lid.

"I'm still hungry," he says, pulling his garage door up just high enough to slip through. "I'm gonna go boil some hot dogs." He disappears into the darkness, and I hear him kick something metal, an oil pan maybe.

The whole walk back to my house, Val is on my mind. It's like all of a sudden I can't wait another second to read her note. At my front door, I realize I don't have my key, so I have to climb through the basement window, which I've done a hundred times. From there, I race up the stairs and into my room, where the jeans I was wearing last night are balled up on a pile of dirty clothes and stuff.

Val's folded note smells like vanilla. I open it, and read.

Hey! Let's do something crazy and fun. I can sneak out if you can. Call me later. —Val

She probably expected me to call her last night, probably thinks I blew her off, plus I never even talked to her today at the picnic. Now Kevin's trying to move in on her, which sucks, but I can't go back to the Kuperskis' now or I'll look stupid, or at least, that's what Charlie would say. If he were here right now, he'd tell me to watch TV for a while, and eat a hot dog, and let Val come to me, so that's what I do. I'm trying real hard not to think about Monday night. I'm trying real hard not to imagine myself alone inside Mareno Chem. But I'm scared.

CHAPTER 10
MONSTERS

IT turns out that a sudden disappearance can make a girl want you more. Val calls me when she gets home from the picnic. I'm passed out on the couch, all tired from eating too much on a hot day, so I don't even hear the phone ring. She leaves a message on our machine. I call her back much later, when it's dark out.

"Can you sneak out tonight?" I ask her, energized from my nap, and heart triple-beating at the sound of her voice.

She laughs, probably because I don't mess around with a lot of small talk. "Why? Where are we going?"

"It's a surprise. Just meet me by the old asphalt plant at midnight."

She says she'll be there. She even says she'll bring some food. I feel an adrenaline rush—not like what I feel when I crash my dirt bike. This is something different. This is something better. I stand in front of my mirror. I mess with my hair for a second. Then I flex my arm muscles. Working out in Charlie's garage hasn't made a huge difference, but my triceps look decent.

A few days ago, at Quick Mart, I caught my reflection in the glass door of a hot dog oven. I kept lifting up my T-shirt and checking out my abs. Then I stood on the edge of the curb and did three sets of calf lifts. Cornpup seemed to be off in his own world, babbling on and on about uranium sludge and whatnot. I didn't think he was paying any attention to me, but I was wrong.

"Why do you care so much about how you look all of a sudden?" he asked me. "You never used to be like that."

"I just want to be strong, is all," I told him. But he wouldn't understand. He could be the strongest guy in Poxton, and he still wouldn't get a girl. Not with his face looking like it does.

It's windy tonight. I stand under a busted streetlight at the edge of the industrial yards. I have on a black sweatshirt and my best jeans. I can't stop moving, jumping in place, kicking little chunks of asphalt. I look in the direction of Val's street, but it's so dark, she could be ten feet away and I wouldn't be able to see her. I turn toward the creek. Tonight the water is alien-green, softly glowing—it couldn't be more perfect. I wish I'd told Val to bring her swimsuit.

"Hey, you." Val sneaks up behind me and puts her arms around my shoulders. "I brought sandwiches and a big bag of corn chips. I forgot something to drink, though."

The last thing on my mind is food.

We climb through a torn section of the chain-link fence. Val snags the knee of her pink exercise pants, but she doesn't make a big deal out of it. We walk to the creek and sit quietly at the water's edge.

"The water is so pretty tonight," she says. "Is this what you wanted to show me?"

I turn on my flashlight and hand it to her. "Hold this for a second. I'll be right back."

Digging with my hands is not an option. I don't want Val to think I'm an animal. I find a fat PVC pipe under some cracked sheets of Plexiglas. I use the pipe to scoop away wet earth until I strike solid wood paneling. It's the doorway to a secret tunnel that leads to more secret tunnels. Charlie and Cornpup would kill me for this.

Val takes one look at what I'm doing and says, "I'm not going in there."

"Why not?"

"It could collapse on us."

"No, wait, look." I point the flashlight at a row of wood joists. "We reinforced all of this. It's totally safe."

Val smiles mischievously. "You're sure?"

"I've been through these tunnels a hundred times."

Some girls would be too weak for this. Some girls wouldn't want to get their clothes dirty. Val is breathing fast, and I can tell she's freaking out, but she climbs into the tunnel with me, and now I like her even more. We crawl through the damp earth for about ten minutes before hitting the jackpot.

"It's an old bomb shelter. From the cold war." I am not totally sure about this, but it *seems* like an old bomb shelter. There's a nuclear symbol on one of the walls.

Val walks over to a pile of private stuff me and my friends can't stash at home. "What's all this?"

If it was anyone else, I'd tell them to back off. Val is picking through Charlie's weapons, tossing saw blades aside, laughing at nunchucks, fake stabbing me with a samurai sword. She shrieks when she uncovers the robot Cornpup built from junkyard scraps.

"Oh my God. Does this thing actually work?"

Of course it works. We load small stones into a chamber on the robot's arm. I tell Val to stand a few feet away. I punch a code into the remote control. The robot fires stones at Val's legs. She laughs so hard, she can't even look at me. When she settles down, she starts picking through our stuff again.

My sketchbooks are wrapped in black garbage bags. She pulls them out gently, like she knows they're special. She doesn't flip through them, half looking, like Charlie would. She goes page by page, studying my drawings like they're the most amazing images she's ever seen.

"I already knew you were an artist. But I didn't know you were this good. You did all this in black pen, but the shading is so perfect, it feels like color."

I shrug and look away. This is a good time to pull out the sandwiches. My hands are dirty, but I don't care. I'm suddenly very hungry.

"What is it with you and monsters?" Val asks me. "Why don't you draw anything else?"

I give her my real answer, the thing I never tell Cornpup and Charlie. "Sometimes I get so pissed off, it's like I'm gonna snap. I pull the anger out of my head and force it into those creatures. Then I feel calm for a while."

Outside the bomb shelter, I hear chunks of earth falling. The tunnels aren't reinforced quite as well as I led Val to believe, but we're still safe. It might be a good idea to get going soon, though, just in case.

Val comes to a two-page illustration of uranium monsters. They're tearing a group of men to shreds. It's my favorite drawing, the angriest picture of all.

"You felt like *this*?" she asks me.

I'm holding a ham sandwich in my dirty hands. I'm chewing a mouthful of dry bread and meat. "Yeah, I felt like that. The night my dad died."

"It was so horrible, what happened to him. I hate to even think about it." Val cocks her head sideways. "These decapitated heads look familiar."

I slide the sketchbook out of Val's hands and toss it to the floor. I don't want to start talking about the Mareno Chem executives. I don't want this night to get ugly. I grab Val's face and kiss her. She kisses me back.

We climb out of the tunnels. I never kissed a girl before tonight. I feel wild and alive. The last time I felt like this was when Charlie brought over a rat in a plastic tackle box. It had scars on its back, little places where its fur wouldn't grow. It jumped out of the box and started running around my bedroom. Cornpup was shrieking, "Bubonic plague! Fleas and ticks! We're gonna get rabies!" And Charlie was saying, "I'll take care of it. I'll catch it. Let me handle it." But I was the one who caught it. I grabbed the rat with my bare hands and threw it outside like it was nothing.

Charlie and Cornpup couldn't believe it.

Tomorrow night, when I'm alone inside the Mareno Chem building, I have to remember this feeling.

CHAPTER 11
MARENO CHEM

THE green-haired monster mask is Charlie's, from last Hallo-ween. The stinky football pads are his too, but they don't fit him anymore. The canister of pesticides came from Cornpup's garage.

"What's all this stuff for?" I ask them. The one thing I've forgot-ten, the one thing I really need, is a watch. We are supposed to be walking to Mareno Chem by way of Two Mile Creek, but we are just standing on the shore, watching the water carry sticks and sludge, beer cans washing up on the rocks.

"Mareno Chem has security cameras. Plus there's a night watch-man on duty," says Charlie. "You're going in there with a mask, some armor, and a weapon. You should be good."

"You're making me more nervous."

"I'm trying to protect you," says Charlie. "Because sometimes you don't think."

He is wrong. All I ever do is think.

"The weapon," says Cornpup, "is the most important thing. Spraying chemicals on a Mareno Chem executive would be poetic, especially if it's the guy who tampered with your dad's safety gear."

"I'm not spraying chemicals on anyone. I just want the jacket back."

"But if someone catches you or tries to hurt you, you have to defend yourself," says Charlie. "Don't be stupid."

"Spray them in the eyes," says Cornpup. "We're talking about the biggest chemical plant in the entire state of New York. We're talking about people who bury toxic drums in neat little rows the way normal people plant corn. They buried your dad. They don't give a damn about us. So let's show them how it feels."

There's a pile of truck tires in the creek. I can't stop looking at all the bald rubber.

Cornpup sees it too. "That right there is why the chemical companies treat our neighborhood like their own personal dumping ground. We're poor. We've got nothing. They think we go around throwing mattresses into the woods and dropping duffel bags full of asbestos tiles into our wells. They don't respect us, because they think we don't even respect ourselves."

Charlie has a strange look on his face. "Why do you always have to say stuff like that? We're not poor. Blue collar isn't poor."

"You can't smell chemicals burning in Buffalo. There's no landfill by the shops on Elmwood Avenue. You get landfills in your town when you don't matter. They throw garbage in your town when they think you're garbage. That's how it is."

I can sense another one of their fights brewing. Charlie is loyal to Poxton, all the more so because this town is like a mangy dog at a pedigree show. It doesn't need a blue ribbon; it just needs someone to love it. Cornpup could not agree less. He says again and again that we *are* poor, that we have been written off.

Charlie lights a match, watches the flame burn down the stick until it reaches his fingertips. Fire is his element.

I think of landfills and dead frogs and creek sludge—these things are everywhere, because industry is everywhere, and without industry, there'd be no jobs. I believe Charlie, who says our lives are normal. When Cornpup refuses to drink Kool-Aid made with our tap water, we say, "Good. More for us." When Cornpup gets talking about toxic air release sirens, we tell him he's putting us to sleep so bad, it's gonna take every toxic air release siren in the world to wake us up.

They cannot get into a fight right now. I won't let them.

I put the monster mask on my head, warty face pointing to the sky, because I need them to remember why we're really here.

It's getting dark fast. I want the sun to stay with us for just a little while longer. I listen for one frog, one cricket, one bird, but living things seem to not like this part of the creek. I sometimes see deer on the mudflats, but it's like there's an invisible barrier; they almost never cross the railroad tracks. Without earthworms, the dirt feels dead in my hands. Without birds, the trees seem like metal sculptures connected by wires that crisscross above my head. Without biting flies, my skin itches anyway, like it has a memory, like it wants to get stung.

Only the rats will survive the dead zone, Cornpup once said to me.

But he was wrong, because there are no rats here.

Mareno Chem looms up ahead. The administration building never fully shuts down. Even now, after hours, it is lit up like a planet—tall streetlights over an empty parking lot; spotlights along the edge of the flat roof; pale fluorescent lights shining through random office windows. There are three rear buildings, each one as dark as death at this time of night: the processing plant, where the chemicals are mixed and contained; the hangar, where chemical trucks and railcars are stored; and the warehouse, where the final products ship out on tankers driven by truck drivers who need hazmat licenses.

"Why isn't Goat's car in the parking lot?" I start to panic. "What time is it? Do you think he bailed on us?"

"He'll be here," says Charlie.

I'm amped up now, scared. "Goat said fifteen minutes, in and out. If I show up wearing this mask, he'll change his mind about the whole thing. He'll say, 'You know what, Hammond, I don't think you're mature enough to go wandering around in the administration building by yourself,' and then I'll really be screwed."

"Just tell me you can run in those shoulder pads without falling," says Charlie. "Save your complaints and excuses for later, because you're gonna owe us big-time if you come out of there alive."

In the end, I put the pads on, even though they're bulky and it's hot out. I wear the monster mask. I carry the canister of bug spray. Having a disguise, armor, and a way to defend myself, well, it's not the worst idea Charlie's ever had.

Goat is waiting at the back employee entrance. He doesn't say anything about my being late, but he does say, "Jesus Christ, Hammond. I've had a bad feeling about this all day, and seeing you in that outfit just makes it worse."

"It's in case they've got security cameras," I tell him.

Goat lets out a long, irritated breath. "All right. Whatever. Here's what you're gonna do."

My stomach knots up.

"You walk down the hallway, just go straight, past the laboratory, and you make your first right. Take the first set of elevators you see. The executive offices are on the third floor. Find your old man's jacket and get the hell out of there as fast as you can. In fifteen minutes, if you're not standing right here, I'm locking you in."

I don't have a watch, I want to tell him, but I'm scared he'll change his mind. He doesn't like me, or what I'm wearing, or the idea of getting his own dad in trouble over my dead father's jacket.

I promise him I'll be quick.

At the edge of the parking lot, Charlie and Cornpup are crouched behind a Dumpster. Cornpup sticks his hand out and waves.

Mareno Chem is beautiful inside. Once I pass the research laboratory with DANGER: AUTHORIZED PERSONNEL ONLY signs posted all over the door, there are contemporary paintings lining the bright white walls. Every office has a glossy metal desk that looks expensive. I catch a glimpse of things sitting at each station: coffee mugs, puppy calendars, framed photos, and pen holders shaped like golf balls. When I reach the elevator, I feel like I want to work in a place like this one day, with my very own desk and important folders.

The third floor is even better. The paintings have golden frames. Real leather chairs are parked at dark wooden desks. None of the potted plants are fake. One guy has a dartboard on his wall, the nice kind, one that lights up and makes sounds. Another guy has a small putting green beneath a window that takes up the entire wall. The pictures on these desks are of families in crisp white shirts and tan pants, standing in front of mansions, waving from cars that are worth more than my house. I like the cruise pictures the most.

I'm not sure how much time has gone by. I haven't been paying attention.

I try to stop getting distracted, but it's hard when everything is so clean and new. I expected the inside of Mareno Chem to be hideous, because of how Cornpup always says chemicals are dirty and chemical workers are monsters.

There's one office left to check, and by the process of elimination, I know exactly who it belongs to: Dan Benecke, vice president and general counsel. He uses his power and his law degree to ruin people. His name is etched on the outside of his door in gold lettering. On his desk there are vacation photos—a cabin at the foot of a ski slope, that leaning tower, fireworks over the ocean, llamas on a footpath in the mountains—all of these trips with the same beautiful woman. It must be wonderful to be a chemical executive, to have no conscience, to live like this.

Behind the desk, a huge map of our town is pinned to the wall. There are red thumbtacks next to our school and the grain mill. There are white thumbtacks in other places, mostly lining the creek. There are notes in sloppy handwriting that I can't read. I wish Cornpup were here. He'd decode this stuff.

There is a red thumbtack stuck in Cornpup's backyard.

I notice a tiny desk clock, gold and polished. It's 9:27. I've taken too long. I might already be locked in here for the night.

Dad's jacket is draped over a chair in the corner.

I pick it up and hold it to my face, breathing in the leather, except I can't smell Dad anymore. I smell this office—coffee and carpet. I smell Charlie's monster mask.

Anger is ripping through me again. I smash the picture frames on Dan Benecke's desk. I tear up his photographs. I use a silver letter opener to slash his leather chair. I scribble MONSTER in black ink all over his desk calendar.

It isn't enough. I want to do more. I want to do something worse.

Instead, I do what I should've done five minutes ago. I speed down the hallway to the elevators, where I press the first-floor button so hard, I jam my finger. I run along the bright white walls, past contemporary paintings and golf ball pencil holders.

All I want to do is get out of this building.

Through the window of the employee entrance, I can see Goat outside smoking a cigarette. Charlie is talking to him, stalling him. I push the door open a crack and hear a sound that's so loud, I feel frozen and confused.

I tripped an alarm.

"What did you do?" Goat shouts at me. "What the hell did you just do?"

He fumbles with his dad's keys and finally, clumsily, locks the door.

Cornpup is at the edge of the parking lot. He points up at red lights flashing all along the top of the Mareno Chem building. "Run!" he shouts.

I have on Charlie's football pads. I'm carrying a monster mask, a can of bug spray, and Dad's jacket. I can't run fast right now. I'm too weighed down and scared.

Goat says to me, "Never again. Don't you ever ask me for anything ever again," and then he takes off in a dead sprint toward the trees.

Charlie says, "Jay, give me the stuff. I'll carry it all. Just run."

When we catch up with Cornpup, the alarm is still squealing. The flashing red lights are obnoxious. There's no doubt in my mind they can be seen from the 990 and beyond.

"We're not walking the edge of the creek home," says Charlie. "It's not safe."

"Which way, then?" I say. "We can't just stay out here. They'll find us. They could bring a helicopter. They could bring dogs."

Charlie looks me in the eye. "You didn't bust any locks. You didn't break any windows. They'll probably do a once-over at the creek, but that's it. They're gonna think this was a false alarm. We'll hide in the tunnels. Twenty minutes after the alarm goes quiet, we'll go home."

Charlie is the best person to be around in a crisis. We follow him to the tunnels.

"What was it like in there?" Cornpup asks.

"It was . . . disgusting," I tell him. Because that's all he really wants to hear.

For some reason, I don't tell my friends what I did to Dan Benecke's office. It feels like it should be something I carry inside me, my secret gift to Dad. Torn photographs. Broken frames. A slashed-up leather chair. I have a small taste of revenge on my lips, and now I want more.

CHAPTER 12
TOWN MEETING

THERE was an explosion at the cold storage plant last night. The blast woke me up. I closed my bedroom window, but I could still smell the fumes. Anhydrous ammonia. My throat is swollen and sore, like I swallowed glass. Chemical throat, we call it. It'll go away in a few hours. I stick a bag of cough drops into my pocket. I don't know what to do about my burning eyes.

We meet at Cornpup's house. Charlie is in a bad mood. "This town meeting is gonna be bad for us," he says. "We don't need a bunch of regulatory agencies hanging around our creek. They'll find our tunnels. They'll confiscate all our stuff. You watch."

Cornpup disagrees. "If the creek belongs to us, then it's our duty to protect it. The EPA can fine corporations thousands of dollars for dumping chemicals into our swimming hole. Think about how good it would feel to see Mareno Chem pay a huge penalty."

I see where Cornpup is going with this, but he's got it all wrong. "You can't punish these guys by going after their money. They've got ways of passing off their losses. They can dump some salaries, lay off a few hundred workers. Or they can claim stuff on their taxes. If we do something to Mareno Chem, it has to cut deeper than money. It has to be bigger and more personal."

Cornpup looks at me, like he knows all about my dark side. "Bigger and more personal can get you thrown in jail, Jason."

Charlie laughs at this. "Maybe, but they'd have to catch us first."

I need to think about something else, something besides revenge. I poke around our Freak Museum and look for new additions. I shake a jar of pink water and it turns tomato-red. I tip a jar of green water upside down, and the solid antifreeze color stays the same, except I've stirred something at the bottom, little fibers that look a lot like orange juice pulp. I look at our bird skeleton and remember how Charlie stepped on a piece of green glass the day we found those tiny bones by the river. No one wanted to pay to see a dead bird, but when I said we had a baby dragon skeleton, we pulled in a dollar per look. A spaghetti sauce jar full of dead bugs wasn't exactly impressive, but I made up a story about a giant insect warrior who hurled beetles from a golden slingshot, and every kid in my neighborhood wanted to buy a dead bug off us.

I never make a big deal out of it, but the Freak Museum should be at my house. I'm the one who brought all these objects to life. I turned a box of scrap metal into UFO parts. I put blood-colored gel and seven cigar stubs into a jar and labeled it *Dead Man's Fingers*. When Charlie found a busted metal cage in a field behind Parish Technologies, I drew pictures of a bubble-skinned beast that chewed through the cage and escaped into the night. When Cornpup dug up an old circuit board, I wrote a story about evil engineers who design weapons using condensed lightning bolts. I even soldered together a mess of canisters, PVC hoses, and television knobs to make one of these "weapons" for the display.

This junk would be nothing without your stories, Cornpup once said to me. But he still keeps the Freak Museum in his bedroom. He still takes all the credit.

"All right. I'm ready." Cornpup is clutching a huge manila folder full of blown-up photographs. He has a rash on the side of his face and looks tired. It's a sweltering afternoon, ninety-seven degrees and holding. Maybe we all look tired.

Charlie takes one look at the folder and says, "No way. You're not bringing all that crap."

Cornpup's voice is scary calm. "Just go home, Charlie. I don't even know why you're here."

For a small second, Charlie seems hurt, but he recovers. "I'll make you a deal. Hit me in the face, and I'll go home. Hit me in the face. Right now. As hard as you can."

It's too hot out for this. If they get into a fight, I'm the one who's going home. There are better things to do. I could be swimming in our creek right now. I could be watching TV.

Cornpup inhales and exhales slowly, like he's hooked up to a machine. I chew a cherry cough drop as loudly as I can. Finally, Charlie wipes the smirk off his face, like even he doesn't have the energy for a brawl today.

He flips through the papers in Cornpup's folder. "Seriously, though. You only get to speak at this meeting for two minutes. Why are you bringing all these pictures?"

I hope Cornpup will recognize this as the peace offering it's meant to be. If Charlie doesn't push you in the chest, if Charlie changes the subject, we're all friends again. No harm, no foul.

"It's all about proof," says Cornpup. "If they say there's no toxic runoff in the creek, I'll show them a picture of ten dead robins floating in liquid asphalt. If they say Phenzorbiflux never existed, I'll show them a picture of a melted squirrel."

"You are *not* bringing up Phenzorbiflux," I say sharply. "We had a deal."

Cornpup won't look me in the eye.

We walk north, toward the Niagara River, sweat pouring down our faces. Charlie carries a football he found at the mudflats. In the sunlight, Cornpup's rash looks blood-red, not purple. I stop at the gas station to buy a bag of pistachios and some Sprite. Charlie and Cornpup wait for me outside.

Kevin Thompson walks in when I'm paying for my stuff. He notices me right away. It doesn't matter to him that the store clerk is watching. He grabs the back of my neck and shoves my face into the counter.

"On the Fourth of July, you're dead," he says. "At the bonfire on Sturgess. In front of Val. In front of everyone."

He lets go of my neck. He tries to talk the clerk into selling him a pack of cigarettes.

I walk outside, a little pissed that Charlie and Cornpup didn't have my back. "How the hell did Kevin Thompson walk right by you guys?"

Charlie looks confused. "He's in the store? Did he see you?"

My face must not look too smashed up. I decide not to tell them he grabbed my neck. "He said he's gonna kill me at Sturgess in front of Val."

"He's all talk," says Cornpup.

"We'll beat the crap out of him," says Charlie.

The town meeting is at Poxton High School. When we reach the parking lot, Charlie says, "There are too many people here. This is too much publicity. They're gonna fence off the creek for sure. It's a done deal."

"Signs and fences can't stop us," I tell him. But I feel nervous. I see a newspaper reporter, people in business suits, unfamiliar faces. I have a feeling things won't be the same for us after today.

I follow Cornpup into the school foyer. There's a table of

refreshments: donut holes and small paper cups of juice. I look at my reflection in the glass trophy case. I seem taller.

Charlie tucks an entire box of donut holes under his arm. Nobody stops him. "You watch," he says. "This is gonna be a freakin' nightmare. We're gonna die of boredom."

"Let's sit up front," says Cornpup.

Charlie gives me a slack-jawed look. "Can this get any worse?"

I recognize some faces, but most of these people have come from beyond Cardinal Drive, from other parts of Poxton, where the Spaulding Fibre plant is scheduled for demolition, where an overturned railroad car dumped a pile of gray mystery dirt into a stream.

Where an elementary school sits at the edge of an unofficial dump site.

My eyes take in the nervous parents with their toddlers. Elderly people walking slowly with their drugstore canes. Men in greasy coveralls. Women in grocery store aprons. Teachers from our old school. I snag my eyes on three chemo-bald people—those shiny heads make me feel so scared sometimes.

The whole auditorium smells like fear.

Yesterday, when we took our skateboards to the Jump, Charlie asked me if I was afraid to die.

"Sort of," I admitted. "But my dad was afraid of death. And his fear didn't protect him."

"Exactly," said Charlie. "Fear takes up all your energy. It screws up your focus. When you're scared, it's easier to make a mistake."

I fell off my skateboard and scraped the hell out of my knee. "What exactly are you trying to say? You think the accident was my dad's fault?"

"No! I'm talking about Cornpup. Ever notice how he *always* brings the conversation back to landfills and toxic sludge? If I tell him I saw a hot girl working at the gas station, he tells me three people on Asher Circle have brain tumors. If I tell him I want to buy a refurbished Camaro someday, he tells me swimming in the creek is gonna alter my DNA. He's not even a real person anymore. He's like a . . . pollution encyclopedia."

Then Charlie did a stupid trick in the air and fell, slicing his shin open on a metal pipe. His skateboard cracked right down the middle.

Today, Charlie's wound is all bandaged up, hidden under his ripped jeans.

Onstage there are six empty chairs and a long table. Representatives from various state agencies appear from behind the velvet theater curtains. They have polite stacks of paper and shiny silver pens. When I see Dan Benecke at the microphone, I'm not exactly shocked. Of course he's here. He has to keep an eye on things. He has to protect Mareno Chem's good name.

"Why is he here?" There is panic in Cornpup's voice. "Why is an industry guy standing up there with the same government people who are supposed to be slapping him with fines? This is wrong. This is so wrong."

Dan Benecke welcomes everyone. He cracks a few jokes. He talks about green initiatives. He talks about jobs. Then he opens the floor for questions and public comments.

"I have a question," Charlie says. "When are you gonna dump more of that cool chunky stuff in the creek? The stuff that smells real sweet like radiator fluid? Because lately you've only been dumping orange foam that smells like cheese. It's been kind of boring."

I elbow him. Hard.

Dan Benecke looks over at us, but he plays it cool. I'm not sure he recognizes me. Does he remember telling Dad to keep his mouth shut or else? Is he proud of how he buried Mom in legal papers, how he forced her to strike a deal? Maybe he doesn't think about us at all. We were loose ends for him to tie up, and now he's planning his next vacation.

Good. Fine. I want him to underestimate me.

I borrow a pen from the lady sitting next to Cornpup. I tear the lid off Charlie's donut box and flatten it, white side up. I begin to draw pictures of giant creek serpents with chemical venom and fangs of broken glass.

There is talk about uranium. Toxic sludge in the creek. They say human exposure is not expected to occur. They say our backyards are safe, but we shouldn't dig holes greater than four feet in depth. They say we shouldn't eat stuff from our gardens. When Dad was alive, he ate tomatoes straight off the vine.

This meeting is full of words. I try to shut it all out, but my ears catch little pieces:

". . . no one really knows . . . into the creek . . . birth defects . . . You people are monsters . . ."

". . . get rid of the waste . . . Why are you ignoring us . . . outrageous . . . hundreds of barrels a day . . ."

". . . poisoned innocent people . . . Please help us . . . I'm not a good public speaker . . ."

". . . We can't leave our homes . . . can't give up our jobs . . . This town is all we have . . ."

". . . You're hiding something . . . many years ago . . . We're sick . . . most of the facilities . . ."

". . . vacant now . . . hazardous waste . . . Don't turn your backs on us . . . People are dying . . ."

People are dying.

I draw a second creek serpent. This one is wearing armor made from exhaust pipes and bike chains. I don't have room to draw a creek serpent battle, so I have to close my eyes and imagine it. Blood and broken fangs and the horrible roar of a serpent warrior.

Cornpup is moving up in line, closer and closer to the microphone. He could say anything. He could say too much.

CHAPTER 13
BUMP SHOW

IT'S Cornpup's turn to speak. They have to lower the microphone for him. I'm running out of blank space on this donut box. I draw a few mud demons, a hawk melting in a puddle of chemical venom, fireworks exploding over a dead serpent's skeleton.

Fireworks. Fourth of July. Sturgess.

I think of Kevin Thompson's empty eyes. Bloody geese. Decapitated ravens. I've got one week till he tries to kill me.

Suddenly I'm not drawing pictures anymore. I am scribbling a solid black patch of ink. I am stabbing tiny holes into the box with the pen tip.

I think about Mom's false start, how she bought produce at the store two weekends ago, even though she's never really been a vegetable eater, even back when she was skinny. I noticed the lettuce right away, a bunch of unfamiliar green stuff. There were tomatoes too, a bag of carrots, red peppers. I waited to see if she'd fix herself a salad. I wanted the vegetables to be the mark of a new beginning, a healthier life, but they rotted away, untouched in that drawer. The smell made me want to punch my fist through a window.

I don't want to be here. But I really don't want to go home.

Cornpup seems a little nervous. He is switching his weight from his left foot to his right foot, like he's trying to hold in a fart. He keeps picking his ear too, and I want to throw something at him to make him stop.

"My name is William Schumacher." He clears his throat. "And I want to show you my skin."

Me and Charlie look at each other. Cornpup never gives a free bump show. He lifts his shirt over his head, and I feel sick inside. I'm not prepared for how bad the bumps have gotten. There are cysts of all sizes pouring down his shoulder blades. The blood-red rash on Cornpup's face stretches beyond his chin, down his neck and right arm. There are white spots on his spine, scars from cysts that were burnt off a long time ago. He is hideous. People gasp and turn their faces away. A newspaper photographer snaps his photo.

"Why is he just standing there?" Charlie whispers. "Why doesn't he say something?"

I shrug. I was expecting one of Cornpup's long sermons, rehearsed right down to the last detail, an angry blue vein popping out of his neck.

Cornpup holds up photographs of horrible things. A mouse with burnt-out eyes. Tumor-covered frogs. Dead trees with black branches. Birds born without any wings.

"It's expensive to dispose of chemical waste in safe ways," Cornpup says. "Mareno Chem saves money when they dump in our creek. They increase profits when they hide barrels of waste in abandoned buildings. No one wants to challenge them. Because of jobs. Watch what happens when Mareno Chem is done using us. Watch what happens when they can't find new hiding places for their waste. They'll close up shop and disappear. They'll leave us here to die."

Dan Benecke doesn't seem worried about anything Cornpup has said. He smiles brightly and says, "I appreciate your comments, son, and I'd like to respond if I may. Mareno Chem is the most environmentally responsible chemical company in the world. We are a leader in green innovation. We budget for safe waste disposal every year. I've seen the numbers. Believe it or not, I was a boy myself once, and I know how fun it can be to imagine a good scandal. But illegal dumping doesn't make good business sense. And when you get to be my age, you'll understand that. Now for our part, we've sealed our drainage pipes as a pledge to this community. We employ hundreds of great people here in Poxton. I'd like to think we're a positive force around here."

So that's how he's gonna play it. He's gonna treat us like we're so cute. Like we've got big, healthy imaginations. Like we're too silly to be taken seriously.

"You're a liar!" shouts Cornpup. "I saw sludge coming out of your drainage pipes last night. I have jars of red water at my house. Green water. You're lying." Cornpup bolts out of the auditorium. I think he might be crying. Me and Charlie run after him. We find him sitting on a generator at the edge of the schoolyard.

"You sounded good in there," I tell him. "The free bump show was a nice touch. You're probably gonna be in the paper."

Cornpup smiles. "You think so?"

A stiff guy in a nice suit approaches us. He says his name is Dr. Gupta, a dermatologist and plastic surgeon from some big hospital in Buffalo. When he asks if he can speak to Mr. Schumacher in private, it takes us a minute to realize that by "Mr. Schumacher" he means Cornpup.

"Whatever you have to say, you can say in front of all of us," Charlie insists.

But Cornpup tells us to please leave.

"What the hell?" Charlie says, all pissed off. "We sat through that stupid meeting, and now he doesn't want us around? Unbelievable."

As we're walking off, I overhear Cornpup and Dr. Gupta engaged in what sounds like a conversation continued from another day. Cornpup says something about surgery and scars. Dr. Gupta says, "Your parents still need to sign the consent forms." Then a truck without a muffler drives through the parking lot, and it's so loud, it drowns out everything else. Now I'm real curious to know what Cornpup's not telling us.

Me and Charlie walk to the shores of Two Mile, because we need to get our clothes muddy. We need to cut our hands open on the sharp rocks. Maybe Charlie will even swallow a mouthful of creek water, because it's a shocking thing to do, and because he knows I've got more cough drops in my pocket.

I know how good it feels, gulping that sharp water, making your throat burn on purpose, never giving in to the tug of fear.

CHAPTER 14
VIPER

TODAY is one of those chilly summer days you get when you live twenty minutes from the Canadian border. Me and Cornpup are sitting on my front porch, freezing our butts off. I watch him tear through today's paper for the fiftieth time, scanning the pages for any mention of the town meeting, and of course, there is none.

"Maybe they'll print it tomorrow," I say, trying to make him feel better. "The reporter was there. He took pictures. Maybe he's just making sure he's got all the facts together or whatever."

Cornpup shakes his head. "No, if they were really gonna run it, they would've done it by now. They're burying the story, like always."

Charlie rolls up on his bike. His ear is heavily bandaged. He's got blacktop skids all up and down his jeans. "I don't want to talk about my ear," he says. "Don't even bring it up."

I notice something wiggling around inside his zipped backpack.

Cornpup is annoyed. "Would it kill you to show up on time? Gramps is on a tight schedule."

We know all about the tight schedule. Pills and a liverwurst sandwich at noon. Nap at one. Forty-five minutes on the toilet at two-thirty. And a mug of warm PBR when the Mets game is on. I hope I never get old.

"How'd your mom do at the farmers' market?" Charlie asks me.

"She didn't buy any vegetables. Or fruit. But she bought three pies. She kept going back for free samples of banana bread till the muffin man told her to move along." I try to make this sound funny, and it is kind of funny—Charlie and Cornpup both laugh—but I feel a little sad.

I don't know why I keep thinking Mom will snap out of her fat-lady phase. I don't know why I keep getting my hopes up.

I watch Charlie's backpack with a vague sense of curiosity. I'm sure I'll find out what's in it soon enough, but the annoying thing is waiting until he's ready to tell us. Charlie won't do anything before he's ready.

We walk past an abandoned plot of land, which has become an unofficial dumping site for ceramic stuff: broken tiles, toilets and bathtubs, fake fireplace logs, and flowerpots. We pass a water treatment plant, a custard shop that will close in the fall, and a warehouse that was once a furniture store. Me and Charlie are trudging along lazily. I kick dandelions like they're soccer balls, leaving behind a trail of decapitated yellow flowers. Charlie rolls several rocks around in his hand, and I can tell he's thinking hard about something. Cornpup is in a major hurry. He's already a couple blocks ahead of us.

I can't stand it anymore. I ask Charlie what's in the backpack.

He stares at one of his rocks, which is really a small chunk of asphalt. "Something."

"Let me see."

"First you have to promise to keep it."

"I'm not promising you anything." To Charlie, promises are permanent, like DNA or a scar. If I promised to cut off one of my fingers, he'd bring the knife.

He unzips his backpack. I see a paw. I see a black tail. "Some guy was selling dogs out on the 990. Labs, purebred, about three months old. My mom's stupid. She doesn't think."

I lift the puppy into my arms. It's a boy dog. He chews my hand playfully. I like dark animals—ravens, panthers, bats, water moccasins—because they match the darkness inside me. But I don't know how to feel about a black dog with a pink tongue and a wagging tail. He's dark and very happy all at once.

Charlie doesn't take his eyes off the dog. "When she got home, she realized you can't raise animals in a house like ours. You can't give my old man something fresh to kick around, some new life to ruin. She tried to return him, but the trailer was gone. The guy took off."

I think about the time Dad bet me five dollars I couldn't catch a chipmunk. I caught a whole boxful, thinking he'd meant five dollars per chipmunk. I wanted to keep them, but Mom said, "Give me a break." I have a feeling she'll be equally annoyed by a puppy.

Charlie touches the dog's face with the kind of tenderness you never see from him.

"Cornpup is too uptight. He doesn't know how to take care of anything but himself. I *need* you to take this dog. I need you to figure out a way to keep him."

Me and my friends, we laugh when we're getting into trouble, when someone farts, when someone slips and falls. But I don't think we really laugh because we're happy. This little dog wags its tail, slobbers on me, licks my face like I'm made of rawhide, and suddenly I'm happy.

"You'll take him?" Charlie asks me.

We walk a little faster, but catching up with Cornpup is no longer an option. He's an angry speck on the horizon.

"My mom doesn't like dogs."

"Don't be stupid. Everybody likes dogs."

We pass a house I've been obsessed with for years. A great horned owl once tried to snatch a baby from the backyard. The baby had deep, infected talon wounds in its skin, but it survived the attack. I sometimes wonder if over the years that kid liked having those unusual scars. I wish I had a crazy feature like that.

Charlie's eyes are a little watery. It's like he's losing a football game on account of a bad call. He feels cheated, because this dog is rightfully his. And he is jealous of me. In his mind, a dead father is probably better than a drunk one with a leather belt.

"Anyway, he's pretty quiet," Charlie says. "Hide him in your room. I'll get you a bowl. I'll get you a bag of food. And here's his leash."

"What's his name?"

Charlie throws a smooth gray rock at a parked truck. Everything is his to ding and dent. He says, "Name him whatever you want. I don't care."

I think of some names, but they don't seem right. I consider *Max* and *Wolverine* and *Spider* and *Dracula*. I consider *Midnight* and *Diablo* and *Raven*. It's easy to come up with a million names and narrow it down to twenty. The hard part is picking just one.

Charlie glances at the plastic bag tied to my belt loop. "Let me get one of those tomatoes," he says. "I'm dying of hunger."

At the farmers' market I used my own money to buy a bag of cherry tomatoes. A pretty farm girl talked me into it. "They're the best in town," she said. "Firm and a little bit sweet." The last time I had a cherry tomato, I picked it from Dad's garden behind the garage. His peppers were underdeveloped, his asparagus stalks were too thin, and his tomatoes were squishy. I don't like eating squishy things. I don't like juices dripping down my hands. If a peach isn't kind of crunchy, I won't eat it. I like bananas when they're still a little bit green.

On the way back from the farmers' market, I asked Mom if she wanted a tomato, and she said, "Get back to me when you have a bottle of ranch dressing."

"But they're good without anything on them," I told her. "They're not like Dad's."

She turned up the radio and said, "Stop talking about tomatoes. You're giving me a headache."

Me and Cornpup ate most of the tomatoes ourselves. We wiped them clean on our shirts. We popped the green stems off with our teeth. I thought about how Dad would've wanted to slice them and serve them with fresh mozzarella and basil. His garden is all dead now. Me and Mom didn't really know how to take care of it.

Mom is gonna kill me if I bring this dog home.

I watch Charlie inhale the rest of my tomatoes. He has an iron gut, I think, because he only has to chew things once or twice before swallowing. I have to chew a lot, or else I get gas.

I put my puppy on the ground so he can bounce around and smell things. "His paws are huge," I say. "He's gonna be a monster."

Charlie tells me Randy and Goat got into a huge fight last night. He tells me Goat got all scared and took off running. The friendship is over. I wonder if this means Randy will act normal again.

I remember the last time I got to hang out with Randy, just me and him, before Goat was even a blip on our radar screen. Mom had fallen asleep at the wheel on her way home from a double shift at the factory. She'd driven Dad's Cutlass into a snowy ditch.

Of course, it wasn't really Dad's car anymore.

When I picked up the phone, I heard her voice, all scared and slobbery. "I almost died tonight. Now the car is stuck."

I was reeling. If it is possible to hate your mom but love her and need her at the same time, then that's what I was feeling. The thought of her getting wiped away forever on a random winter night filled me with raw fear. Charlie was sprawled out on my couch with no intention of getting up. He was finishing off an entire box of Triscuits. "Call Randy. He'll drive you out there," he said without taking his eyes off the TV.

Riding on the back of Randy's motorcycle wasn't what I thought it would be. He made me wear a helmet. He took the icy curves real slow. Mom was shaking when we got there.

"I almost hit that tree," she said, pointing.

Randy flashed his Pellitero smile, calm and confident. "You're fine. You're alive. We don't need to know all the stuff that didn't happen."

I let Mom hug me while Randy got the car up onto the road. "I thought we were gonna need a tow, but I guess not," he said. "Are you okay to drive home?"

Mom joked, "I'm wide awake now."

"Then we're going to make one stop before we swing by your place," Randy told her.

We followed Mom's car till she turned off 290. Then we drove to Wendell's Diner, where Randy bought me a huge piece of pecan pie with ice cream on it. I didn't want pecan pie, because I like apple, but he kept saying, "You gotta try it. Seriously, just try it," so I did.

Molly McVie was our waitress. She was supposed to have died five years before, leukemia or something, but she miraculously recovered. I remember thinking she was the prettiest girl in Poxton. I remember thinking that's why she got to live, because the grim reaper fell in love.

"I'm gonna marry her someday," Randy told me.

I believed him. The Pelliteros always get what they want. They set their eyes on a girl or a touchdown, and everybody else might as well quit.

I didn't mind that Randy ate most of my pie. It didn't bother me when he was whispering stuff into Molly's ear. It felt good, knowing things about Randy that Charlie didn't know.

A few months later, when Goat came on the scene, Randy turned mean. He had a new girl on the back of his motorcycle every weekend. Sometimes he whipped beer cans at our heads.

Charlie loops his finger through a hole near the collar of his faded Bills T-shirt. He takes a deep breath and says, "Randy's in love or something. Goat kept making nasty comments about his girl, kept jabbing him, trying to start something. So Randy smashed his face."

"Wish I could've been there to see that," I say.

We climb Gramps's wooden porch steps. I carry my puppy close to my chest. Charlie rings the doorbell.

The Mets game is blasting from an old radio—two outs, bottom of the first, runner on second. We hear shuffling. We hear an old man coughing. We hear what sounds like a person tripping over a cardboard box. The door flings open. Gramps has a crazed look in his eyes, white hair and long eyeteeth, brown spots all over his skin. "Oh. It's you."

Charlie laughs. "Who'd you think it would be?"

"Jehovah's Witnesses. They won't leave me alone."

Cornpup greets us from the living room, where the sticky floor is pulsing with ants. He looks at me and says, "Why do you have a dog?"

"Charlie gave him to me."

Cornpup doesn't feel like he got passed over. He wants a dog even less than I want to watch Mom enter a hot dog eating contest. He has the Freak Museum to take care of. A dog could chew up something toxic and irreplaceable. "You should call him Rocky," he says.

"No," I say, shaking my head. "I was thinking Viper. His teeth are real sharp."

Charlie smiles a little. He approves.

Me and Charlie sit on the couch. Cornpup is pouring maple syrup onto the floor, which is something he's done every Friday for as long as I can remember, because Gramps needs traction when he's shuffling around, and God forbid he use a walker.

It catches us all off guard when Gramps turns off the Mets game and grabs Cornpup by the throat.

CHAPTER 15
SHOCK

THE argument is hard to follow. Gramps says something about experimental surgery. Cornpup says something about Dr. Gupta, who knows how to make burn victims look a lot better than lizards, who understands skin the way steelworkers understand hot metal. Gramps says Cornpup is gonna end up deformed. And Cornpup says, "Look at me. I'm already deformed." They shout back and forth about detox tea, skin cream, and the difference between a plastic surgeon and a witch doctor. Gramps says there's no way Cornpup's mom is gonna give him two hundred dollars. And Cornpup says he just needs her to sign the consent forms; he'll find a way to come up with the money on his own.

Me and Charlie look at each other. Cornpup has been hiding things.

It's hard to breathe in this stuffy room, surrounded by maple syrup and piles of random junk. There is a tuba in the kitchen sink, a heap of books spilling out of the coat closet, a gooey pile of Scrabble squares and Monopoly hotels at my feet. Viper is the only peaceful thing. He just met me today, and already he is sleeping soundly in my lap.

Gramps shuffles across the sticky floor. No one would ever look at him and think, *Steelworker, lost two fingers saving another man's arm, could work an open-hearth furnace in his sleep.* "I'm not paying you to do the syrup anymore. If you want to stop coming here, that's fine. At least you know where I stand."

Cornpup drops the syrup tub. He looks up at us, like he's just now remembering we're here. He says, "I'm getting my skin fixed for real this time. And no one is going to stop me." Then he runs out the door.

I wish I had a pencil and a piece of scrap paper. I'd sketch a picture of Gramps as a carnivorous plant, growing out of a steel bucket of maple syrup.

"He's a fool," Gramps says to us. "I know you boys think you know everything, but experimental surgery is no joke. He could *die*. For what? For pretty skin! And you two are no better. Self-absorbed fools is what you are."

Charlie says, "You don't know us. You don't know anything about us," and storms out the front door.

Now me and Viper are stuck dealing with Gramps, who is clearly insane. I would explain our world to him, but he would never understand. We cross a landfill on our way to school. We swim in creek water that smells like nail polish remover. Charlie can convert a third and twenty-six situation into a touchdown. I can create a world of uranium monsters and blind creek serpents on a sheet of blank paper. Cornpup can transform a pile of broken metal parts into a four-foot-tall robot. We are not fools. We are brave and brilliant.

Gramps touches my arm. There are tears in his eyes. "Will you talk to him for me?" he says. "Will you tell him not to do the surgery?"

"I don't know. Maybe." I stand up and turn the Mets game back on. Three balls, one strike, no outs. There are two runners on base. I feel like I can't get away from this place fast enough. When I walk outside, Cornpup is nowhere in sight. Charlie is carving *I hate you* in Gramps's porch steps with his army knife. "Race you home," he says.

We break into a hard run. The weight of Viper in my arms slows me down a little, but I am only two steps behind Charlie's heels. My legs are getting stronger. Charlie hops an overturned garbage can and stumbles into the grass. We start laughing our heads off then, and I think there is nothing that feels better than a fast run.

Bang. A muffler backfires at the end of the street. All I can think of is dead seagulls falling like rain. Tomorrow night there will be fireworks on Sturgess. Kevin Thompson wants to push me into the bonfire. He wants to see me burn.

When I say I want to walk to Cornpup's house, Charlie refuses to come along. He's pissed about the secret surgery plans. He needs time to cool down.

I think I'll try to talk Cornpup out of the surgery, but not because of anything Gramps said. I've got my own bad feeling about this. Some big-shot doctor shows up out of the blue and wants to put Cornpup under anesthesia so he can cut him up at no charge. It sounds shady.

Mrs. Schumacher opens the door and says, warily, "He's in his room." Then she goes back to watching TV. I climb the stairs and stand outside Cornpup's bedroom, my hand ready to knock, when I hear sobbing worse than how I wept, biting my pillow in the dark, the night Dad died. He is snorting, hiccupping, moaning. His sadness is like static electricity, shocking my hand when I touch the door. I feel like I'm doing something wrong, like I'm violating his privacy in a big way. When he gasps for air, I suddenly, finally, understand what this means to him. He wants this surgery the way I want Dad back.

I walk down the stairs and out the door. I've made a decision. I'm gonna help him.

I have to help him.

But first, I have to sneak a puppy into my house.

CHAPTER 16
BONFIRE

ON Sturgess, there is a patch of fenced-off coal ash, as fine as sand. Everybody is barefoot, shoes piled high in a pit of cement blocks, because it's tradition to pretend this is a beach bonfire, that the dark industrial yard is really a raging ocean.

We show up carrying things that will burn. Charlie has a bag of foam egg cartons. I have a can of paint and some cracked wooden paneling we found in my garage. Cornpup is carrying five newspapers and a long, heavy chain.

"What's that for?" Charlie asks him.

"I found it at the railroad tracks," Cornpup says. "I'm gonna climb that huge tree for real this time."

"Shut up," I say. "No one can climb that."

"You need a rope, not a chain," Charlie points out. "Or you'll fall in the fire."

"What I *need* is motivation. When there's a bonfire underneath me, falling isn't an option."

Bang. I close my eyes and see a cardinal buried in a Dumpster.

Kevin Thompson wants to kill me tonight. In front of Val. In front of everyone.

I need to calm down.

"Who picked out this crappy music?" says Charlie. "My *grandma* listens to soft rock. Where's the hard stuff?"

"Change the station, then!" someone says.

I scan the crowd for Kevin. I don't think he's here yet.

"If something happens to me tonight, will you take Viper back to my house?" I ask Charlie.

He looks at me like I'm crazy. "What are you even talking about? Let's just have fun."

There are a hundred kids here, easy, their faces glowing in the orange light. I pay close attention to the girls who sit on lawn chairs and broken television sets near the fire. I wonder when Val and her friends will show up.

I thought I could be brave, but my hands are shaking a little.

Charlie hijacks the radio, hooks it onto a low branch, and cranks up a heavy metal station. When the wind blows, the radio bobs up and down, dangerously close to the flames. His popularity is crazy at events like this, where even kids from other schools seem to know who he is. He takes a whole bag of Starbursts away from some girl, and she seems *happy* about it, probably thinking he's flirting with her, when those who know him best would say he's just being rude.

The fire is melting a box of plastic ice cube trays. The smell of the smoke makes me thirsty. Cornpup is off in his own little world, still trying to toss his stupid chain up into the tree—we are pretty much ignoring him now. Well, Charlie is ignoring us both. I hate standing on the edge of a party, blending into the shadows, but I've been following Charlie around for the last half hour, and he hasn't said a word to me. I'm supposed to be his *best friend,* but I sense something intentional here, like he's trying to exclude me just because he can. I'm glad I brought Viper. Dogs let you be alone without being *alone.* When Charlie is done making his rounds, he'll bring me a can of pop, and he'll say, "Where have you been? I've been trying to find you for, like, an hour," which won't be the truth.

Someone brought beer, even though it's not supposed to be that kind of a party. I watch Robby Carter cough with disgust after a skunky sip, but he doesn't drop the can. He's an idiot for drinking something he doesn't even like. He should fake it, like I do, taking a pretend sip every five minutes or so, then "losing" the can somewhere. No one's paying enough attention to notice.

Charlie gets loud and hyper as more people show up. He feeds off the energy of a crowd. He has on a huge leather jacket that doesn't even fit right, and it's the hottest night of the year. But he is king. It's like this bonfire is blazing for him. The rest of us, we're just props.

I grab a can of pop from the cooler. A pretty girl with really nice blond hair scratches Viper under his chin. Someone throws my paint into the fire. It burns really good, except there is now a dizzy smell in the air. I look for Cornpup at the base of his infamous tree, but he's gone. I sit down, pressing my spine against the knotty trunk. Viper is beside me, curling his body into the root system like it's a dog bed.

"Get up, Hammond." That voice, it hits me like a gunshot.

So this is it. I stand up.

"Can't we do this some other time?" I say in a bored voice. "Do you really want to be the guy who kills someone at Sturgess? Do you really want to be the reason the cops come out here and shut this party down?"

"Hell yeah, I want to be that guy." Kevin punches me in the stomach. Hard.

That's my plan? To talk my way out of this? To reason with an insane person? Wonderful.

I ball my hand into a fist, ready to pound his face in. I swing and miss.

"Your fat pig mom won't recognize you when I'm done," Kevin says.

I feel knuckles cracking against my jaw. I drop Viper's leash to the ground. I wonder what happened to my anger, the inner explosion that rocks me awake at night, the rage I channel into my drawings. Where is that power when I really need it? Why can't I move a single muscle—to block a punch, or to run away, or at the very least to reach for Viper's leash so he doesn't wander off into the darkness?

"Fight back!" Kevin shouts at me.

I check and make sure Viper is still at my feet, and he is. But that one wasted second leaves me open to another hard punch, again to the stomach.

I hear a girl's voice say, "Oh my God."

The grain mill. The trucks. The spray paint. I want to tell him it wasn't all me. It wasn't *my* idea.

An iron chain drops slowly into my line of vision. There's a big hook at the end that makes me think of shipyards, gantry cranes. It inches down, behind Kevin's head, without a sound—he has no idea it's there. I wait for someone to warn him, but no one does.

The chain drops lower. I wonder what Cornpup is planning to do.

Kevin says, "Stop embarrassing yourself. Fight back."

Cornpup swings the chain. He tries unsuccessfully to hook Kevin's sweatshirt. He swings the chain, and misses his target again. His plan isn't as brilliant as I hoped it might be. I inhale a deep breath of smoky air. I taste paint fumes in the back of my throat.

Kevin is shouting at me, words and threats, but what I hear is

Bang. Long pause. *Bang.* Long pause. *Bang, bang.* He pushes my shoulders. I fall back against the tree. He then leans down, his face real close to mine, and he says, "You're making this too easy."

I look up and see Valerie, who is watching me with a concerned—no, *horrified*—look on her face. I smile at her a little bit, and Kevin thinks I'm asking for more. He is about to kick me in the stomach, when the hook finally catches. Cornpup pulls up on the chain, and Kevin is jerked into the air, two feet off the ground, just like that. I laugh out loud because Cornpup isn't strong enough to lift a person. He must've rigged a pulley system or something.

Kevin screams like a girl. I wait for his sweatshirt to rip, but it doesn't. Cornpup raises the chain again, until Kevin is looking down at me. I gotta hand it to the guy, he's still trying to hit me, but I can dodge him now. I am quick again. I am no longer frozen. I grab Viper's leash. I look at Kevin for a long time, feeling mostly pity. He stares back at me with only hate. "We're on fucking food stamps because of you," he says.

Bang. I close my eyes and see a raven that did not die, a raven that is flying, unharmed.

"I can trump your food stamps," I tell him. "My dad is dead."

Charlie pushes his way through the crowd. "What the hell is going on?"

Kevin's sweatshirt finally gives, and he falls hard onto his stomach. His face hits the dirt.

His forehead is less than a foot from the fire. I see a flash of silver, a knife strapped to his belt loop. He jumps to his feet.

I hear people laughing. I hear people taunting him. Valerie is smiling big. They all assume me and Cornpup planned this, that I took punches not because I froze at the worst possible time but because I was drawing Kevin in, forcing him to move closer to the hook. I think people see what they want to see, because no way did we look coordinated just now. This was a total fly-by-the-seat-of-our-pants operation, the kind of thing that only looks cool because it actually worked. I can picture about ten different scenarios where things would not have gone so well for me, but if Randy were here, he'd flash a calm, confident smile and say, "We're fine. We're alive. We don't need to know all the stuff that didn't happen."

The first fireworks explode in the distance—buzzing red lights, golden weeping willow trees, bursts of blue spheres.

Kevin takes off running. I don't know where he's going. I don't care.

"I missed it," Charlie says, louder this time. "What happened? Did he *hit* you?"

I ignore him on purpose, just so he can know how it feels for once. People line up to talk to me—football players, guys from the hockey league, cute girls. It's like I'm famous, even though I didn't actually *do* anything.

"Cornpup's the one you should be talking to," I say. "He's the one who hooked him."

I am glad when the attention shifts away from me. I don't pretend to be more interesting than a sky full of fireworks.

Valerie touches my shoulder. Her eyes are blue and green, always changing. "I'm glad you didn't hit him," she says. "I'm glad you're not like that."

It is the perfect moment for a kiss—the soft glow of a bonfire, a sky filled with fireworks, the exhilaration of having lived through a fight I've been dreading. I lean in, and she leans in, but no . . . instead of a kiss, there's a chain rattling between us.

"I'm hungry," Cornpup says. "Toss me up something spicy. Preferably an unopened bag of Doritos."

"I'll be right back," I say to Valerie. She holds Viper's leash for me.

I feel so alive, I almost believe fire could never hurt me, that I'm invincible, like Charlie. Tonight would be a great night to destroy Dan Benecke. Tonight would be a good night to take down Mareno Chem. But there will be other nights.

Right now, I just want to kick back and enjoy the fireworks.

CHAPTER 17
GOLDEN NUGGET

CHARLIE says he knows where the Phenzorbiflux is hidden. This time he's sure. He says he had a dream about it. A dream that was so real, he tasted fumes in his throat when he woke up. It's a ten-mile trip to the shores of Lake Erie. We ride our bikes in silence.

The lake is covered in a dark, oily sheen. Charlie thinks it would be awesome to see the water catch fire. He wants to watch container ships sailing through the flames, blankets of smoke engulfing the historical lighthouse, dead fish washing onto shore. I imagine the monsters that could crawl out of a burning lake—screaming seagulls with fire wings, toxic squid that glisten in the night, smallmouth bass with steel spikes welded to their fins.

We leave our bikes by the water. We walk along the railroad tracks to the old Bethlehem Steel mill. It's a massive compound, more than a mile long, and totally abandoned. Back in World War II, steelworkers rolled uranium here. They were helping to build the bomb that got dropped on Hiroshima. They didn't know they were supposed to wear protective gear. Some of them took little pieces of uranium home to their kids. People got radiation poisoning. And cancer. Some of the buildings are still hot. And the soil here will stay contaminated for thousands of years.

"This doesn't look anything like my dream," says Charlie. He describes a building that could be any one of these.

"There are a lot of warehouses with busted windows," I say. "Can't you narrow it down?"

He cannot.

I wonder if Charlie's dream was only half true. Maybe Mareno Chem workers did come here, but not to *hide* Phenzorbiflux. Instead they might've shipped the secret chemical out on railcars that passed through here. Or maybe they parked their tankers on Bethlehem Steel property and poured every last trace of Phenzorbiflux straight into Lake Erie.

Charlie kicks an old diesel tank and says, "Goddammit."

The truth is, I'm starting to burn out. I'm tired of searching for Phenzorbiflux. There is too much ground to cover. There are too many places where liquid chemicals can be soaked into soil or washed out to sea. It could take us years to break into every possible building, to dig through hundreds of square miles of earth, and we still might not find what we're looking for. If we prove Phenzorbiflux is real, if we prove it was manufactured here in Poxton, we'd silence all the people who say Dad was a liar. And Mareno Chem would probably get in trouble with the government, which would be great.

It's just that Mareno Chem doesn't have a face or a heart. It can't feel pain. I need to direct my anger at an actual person. I need to seriously hurt Dan Benecke. It's almost all I can think about.

We leave Bethlehem Steel with failure in our guts. It's a long ride home.

"Let's stop back at your place and pick up Viper," says Charlie. "Then we should go see my brother. He'll give us free drinks."

I remember when I had to draw three skeleton posters for Randy's twentieth birthday party. Charlie wanted almost every bone in the human body to be represented, which took forever, and then he wanted me to "kill" each of the skeletons in a different way. So I drew one skeleton drowning in the ocean, a school of tropical fish swimming through its ribs. I drew the second skeleton lying on a flat stone, a tribe of cannibals picking bloody flesh off its spine and rib cage. And I drew the last skeleton in a dark, dirty factory, a hydraulic pressing machine crushing one arm into jagged shards of bone.

When Randy saw the posters, he said, "You should do something with your art. Like work on movie sets in Hollywood."

I kind of love that idea. I could do special effects for monster movies. I could design creatures. I could put zombie makeup on a famous actor's face. I have no idea where I could get trained for that type of job.

We all thought Randy would be in college by now. He's a talented quarterback, a quick guitar player, but no scholarships were offered to him, and Charlie says, "In this town, you gotta get a scholarship or you're done. Our parents ain't giving us any college money. We're on our own." Randy applied for work at the lumberyard, at a fuel processing facility by the river, and at the air products plant where Mom works. He wanted to drive a forklift at the shipyard. He thought about doing some roofing work in the summer. "Good luck," Mom said to him. "Because nobody's hiring these days. And I mean nobody." Right now Randy is working behind the snack counter at the Golden Nugget, and it's just temporary, till he can find something better.

When we get to my house, Charlie rummages through our pantry, and takes a bag of pretzel sticks for the road. I secure Viper in my backpack, so he can see everything without falling out while we ride. Then we hop on our bikes and head out past the industrial yards, toward the Canadian border.

"Bingo is the greatest thing ever," says Charlie. "The cash-in prize is two hundred dollars for a regular game, three hundred for a blackout. *In one day* we could win Cornpup all the money he needs for his stupid skin creams. Except you gotta be eighteen to play. Can you believe that garbage?"

"So you're not mad at him anymore? You're okay with the surgery?"

Charlie shakes his head. "If my skin looked like that, I'd get the surgery in a heartbeat. I was never really mad about that. I was just pissed he was being so top-secret."

The Golden Nugget doesn't actually open till noon, but we pound on the tinted glass windows at eleven-thirty, and Randy lets us in. "Just don't let my boss see that dog," he says to me.

Molly McVie is sitting at the bar, a paperback novel open in her lap. She has on tiny pearl earrings and a strapless pink sundress. Her blond hair is pulled into a ponytail. There is something so hot about the curve of her shoulders, all soft-looking and tan. Randy almost spills a tub of popcorn kernels all over the floor because he's watching her and not the kettle.

So he finally got the girl he always wanted.

Molly smiles at us. I wonder if she remembers me from that snowy pecan pie night at the diner. The night me and Randy were like brothers. The night Mom slid off the road.

"They're always together. It's sickening." Charlie is one of those people who could live forever off teriyaki beef jerky, macaroni and cheese, and a regular rush of adrenaline. When it comes to girls, he likes the thrill of the chase, but what he *loves* is freedom. I don't know if he'd ever want a real girlfriend. He likes Jill, I guess, but she's second-tier; he'd choose sports, pepperoni pizza, and Chemical Mountain over her any day of the week.

"Having Molly around is better than seeing Goat's ugly face," I say. "Plus Randy's back to normal now."

Behind the bar there are three rows of candy boxes, two clear bins full of tortilla chips, and a nacho cheese dispenser. Cheese-filled hot dogs rotate under a small lightbulb. The last time I ate a cheese-filled hot dog, I threw up at the Erie County Fair.

Charlie dumps a baggie full of change onto the counter. "How much can we buy with this?"

Randy laughs. "That'll maybe get you some M&M's off the floor."

I haven't been hungry since my close call with Mom this morning. I woke up to her violently jiggling my door handle. "Why is this door locked? What are you doing in there? Open up, now." I shot out of bed. I tucked Viper under a deflated rubber raft and some mildewed towels. I unlocked my door. Mom stormed in to conduct a quick search. Maybe she thought I was doing drugs. Viper was motionless and quiet the whole time. I thought for sure she'd notice little black puppy hairs all over my pillowcase, but I was saved by the overall messiness of my room—railroad spikes and scrap metal on the floor, dirty shirts and underwear in a smelly heap, monster sketches stuck to the walls with gum.

"No locked doors," Mom said. "That's the rule."

And then she left for the air products plant, her van squealing down the street. To Cornpup, that sound is a serpentine drive belt that needs to be replaced. To me, it's the sound of freedom: She's gone.

But sooner or later, she's gonna discover Viper. Every time I think about it, I totally lose my appetite.

Randy gives us two tall paper cups filled with ice and Mountain Dew. "On the house," he says.

"So what's up with you and Valerie?" Charlie says to me. "I heard she's been knocking on your window in the middle of the night."

"No comment." I chew my plastic straw until it's mangled.

"Val and Jill want us to take them on a double date," says Charlie.

The popcorn kettle is too noisy, one hundred bullets in a tin can. Viper doesn't like it.

"What are you guys talking about?" Molly moves closer to us. I watch her purse slide along the shiny counter.

Please, oh please, sit next to Charlie.

She sits next to me.

Randy glances at the wall clock. Three minutes until he has to unlock the front doors. He puts out a cup for tips. He checks out his triceps in the mirrored wall. He can do one-armed pull-ups, which is amazing. I don't wish I could be him. I want to be myself, except with his looks, his confidence, and his ability to play guitar riffs, quick fingers flying up and down the frets of an electric Les Paul. I wouldn't mind having his motorcycle either.

"Jason has a *girlfriend*. Valerie Tennyson," Charlie explains.

"Not true," I say. Sitting next to Molly makes me feel itchy. She smells like peaches. Valerie sometimes smells like vanilla. I liked my life a lot better when girls were gross and dead frogs were beautiful. Now everything is so complicated.

"You're not going on no date," says Randy. "You don't have any money. You don't have a car."

"I'll steal Dad's truck," says Charlie.

Randy laughs out loud. "You're crazy. He will *kill* you. Why don't you just have them over for tacos or something?"

It's time for Randy to unlock the front door. We watch old people flooding the bingo hall. Saggy arms, dentures, gambling visors, and polyester. I catch a whiff of expired perfume that makes my stomach turn. I wonder if it's a rule that old people have to dress old and smell old.

"I thought up an idea last night," I tell Charlie. "A way we could get Cornpup some of the money he needs."

Charlie is holding a book of matches. He strikes them, one by one, watching the flames burn and then disappear.

Molly says, "Charlie and fire, now that's scary."

CHAPTER 18
PLANS

THE first bingo game is under way. A man in the announcement booth calls out, "B-two, G-nine, B-eleven, I-nine, O-three." The players are in deep concentration. They do not talk to each other. They do not look up. There is only the furious dabbing of numbered squares.

I think about eating tacos with Valerie, Jill, and Charlie. It would be so weird. Valerie's skinny, with tiny bones like a bird. I bet she'd only eat one taco, while me and Charlie, we'd eat five or six. And then she'd probably want to hold my hand or something. I can see it now, me with a piece of cilantro stuck between my teeth, and Charlie flicking shreds of cheese into Valerie's long, dark hair.

I don't know if I really want Charlie to be there when I hang out with Valerie, because he might tell her things about my fat mom, or he might make up a lie about me that's meant to be a joke but won't be taken that way, like the time he told Cornpup I fart when I run fast, which is not true. On the day we had class pictures, Charlie got pizza sauce all over my good shirt, and I swear it was on purpose.

He's the friend I hate and the friend I love, all mixed into one person. .

"Hey, Fire Starter," I say. "Do you want to hear my plan or what?"

Charlie doesn't even bother looking up from his matches. "It won't work."

"You don't even know what I'm gonna say!"

"It doesn't matter what you're gonna say. There is no way we can raise two hundred dollars for Cornpup before school starts. Not legally, anyway."

I hesitate. Suddenly I'm not sure my idea will sound as good out loud as it did in my head last night. "I was thinking we could do a Freak Tour."

Charlie makes a face.

"Just hear me out. Every piece in the Freak Museum has its own story. Each story happened somewhere. So we take a group of kids to the field of barrels and we tell them it's a war zone where the robot battles took place. And then we take them to the tunnels we dug, where crazy scientists are hiding robots; and to the steel mill, where a ghost is still looking for his glass eye; and to the rubber factory, where giant rats stalk and eat humans."

"We're not showing anyone our tunnels," says Charlie.

"Wait, why does Cornpup need two hundred dollars?" Randy has a confused look on his face. "I thought some doctor is gonna fix his skin for free."

I explain how Cornpup is gonna have to take care of his body after the surgery. "The doc says he'll need to apply expensive creams four times a day, plus he'll have to take herbal pills and drink detox tea. Otherwise the cysts could come back."

Randy mutters something about the doctor being a scam artist.

119

Charlie says my idea could work. "You know that wooded area by the tracks, kind of by all those railcars?" he says. "I found a cold patch of dirt about ten feet wide—"

"The cold spot!" Molly interrupts him. "I've been out there. You're walking along, and it's a hot summer night, and then suddenly you feel this frozen ground right under your feet. No animals around, not even bugs. It's like a dead zone. Maybe you could think up a story for that."

"It's where the ice monsters live," I say. "In underground cities."

Molly says, "Wow. That was fast."

Charlie says, "That's nothing. Wait till you see his sketchbook."

"What about the water in the creek?" Randy asks. "You got a story for that too?"

"Depends on the color," I tell him. "Red is goblin pee. Green is alien blood."

Now Randy laughs. "That's actually pretty hilarious."

They ask me how much I'm gonna charge for the tour. I don't know. Charlie says the tickets should be cheap, because little kids never have any money. Molly says there's no reason why we should limit this to just little kids. I tell her we're *absolutely* limiting this to little kids, because the tour will cover every no trespassing zone from here to the 990, and I don't want to deal with police officers, lawsuits, phone calls to parents, or any other adult complication. Randy says I have a good point. Charlie lets it slip that we've got a bloody flannel and a shoe box full of dead bats in the Freak Museum. Molly says the bloody flannel sounds disgusting and we should be careful because bats carry rabies. And then Randy is back on the subject of tickets, which he thinks should be expensive, since the Freak Tour is a once-in-a-lifetime event.

"Bingo!" shouts a woman with tubes in her nose. She can't get up to show her ticket, because she's strapped to an oxygen tank with Canadian flag stickers all over it. The announcer leaves his booth and walks over to check her card. She wins two hundred dollars. She waves a pink dabber above her head, and a few people applaud lamely. Game two begins.

"Cornpup charged two dollars for a trip to the incinerator back when all the frogs died," says Charlie. "A ticket to his Freak Museum costs maybe four bucks. So we charge three dollars for the tour and a buck-fifty for a book of stories."

"What book of stories?" Viper is getting restless. He stands in my lap. I don't want Randy's boss to see. I try to cover him with my bag, but you can still tell he's there. I press down on the base of his tail, trying to get him to sit, but he fights me. We'll have to leave soon.

"The one you're gonna write," Charlie tells me.

Whoa. Wait a minute. I never said I was writing any book.

"You get twenty kids, and you'll make close to a hundred dollars," says Randy. "Not bad."

Charlie pushes his cup away. He walks toward the door without saying goodbye to anyone. Typical. I climb off my stool, thank Randy for the free soda, and clip Viper into his harness.

Charlie is fidgeting at the door. "Hurry up. Hurry up. Hurry up."

"Wait." Randy doesn't shout this to Charlie. He says it quietly, to me.

I turn back to the counter. Charlie lets out a loud, impatient sigh.

Randy says, "I think the Freak Tour is a real good idea. But I'm not so sure Charlie should be volunteering you to write out an entire book of landfill stories. That's a lot of work. If you decide to do it, then sure, yeah, throw a little money Cornpup's way. Just swear to me you'll keep something for your trouble. It's important to look out for yourself."

So this is what it feels like to have a big brother, someone who cares about my best interests. Cornpup might help me assemble the books, and I bet Charlie will promote this thing till kids are beating down my door for tickets, but Randy's right. Most of the work will fall on me. I'll have to write out all my stories. And the illustrations will take forever to draw. Maybe I *should* get something out of this.

When I was really little, like six or seven, I found a wad of cash out by the loading docks. I thought it was a million dollars, but it was probably more like fifty. I kept the money in an empty plastic margarine tub under my bed for weeks before I finally showed it to Charlie. He said a plastic margarine tub was too risky. He told me he'd keep the money safe for me in his lockbox. I never saw that wad of dollar bills ever again. It doesn't matter that I had no idea what to spend fifty dollars on, or that Mom probably would've found that money and used it for groceries. What matters is that I let Charlie call the shots. I always have.

I leave the air-conditioned Golden Nugget and catch up with Charlie in the parking lot. I take my shoes off and step barefoot on the hot pavement. I let Charlie walk Viper for a while. We are sweating, and Viper is panting, and no cool breezes come to us from the north. The sun won't set for hours, won't even touch the tree-tops until after seven.

"Let's ride the landfill tonight," says Charlie. "Tomorrow we'll start planning the Freak Tour."

I was thinking the exact same thing.

CHAPTER 19
CHEMICAL MOUNTAIN

CORNPUP has the best basement. His dad buys used pinball machines from taverns that go out of business, and there's a jukebox that looks old-fashioned but plays hard rock music, and there's a spare freezer stocked full of pizzas and stuff. The only bad thing is, we have to put up with his little sister, Abbi, who runs around the pool table, screaming, with three dolls strapped upside down in a plastic stroller, until Charlie says, "Please, Cornpup, there must be a soundproof closet we can lock her in. Just for a little while." Now she's upstairs having dinner, which means it's late. The Schumachers never eat before dark.

We got sidetracked. Charlie and Cornpup are shooting pool, and I'm playing the monster pinball machine, racking up thousands of points, because I've figured out how to get the ball to roll up into the mummy's eye, and then down a long, neon green tube, before landing in the vampire's outstretched hand. When I'm on a hot streak like this, Charlie won't play me.

"What time is it?" Charlie asks.

I have a high score, twenty-two thousand points.

Cornpup runs upstairs to check. He yells down to us, "Nine forty-five. And there's a tornado warning. It's real windy."

"Good," says Charlie. "Let's go."

Cornpup says I can stow Viper in the basement while we're gone, which is a relief. I'm still not sure it's safe to leave Viper alone in my bedroom. He could whimper, and Mom would find him, and then I'd be in major trouble. I give Viper a beef-flavored bone and make a dog bed out of Cornpup's army-green sleeping bag. "I'll be back in a little while," I say. "Be good."

When me and Charlie get upstairs, Cornpup has on a trench coat, a knit cap, and a pair of rubber dishwashing gloves.

"It's not that cold out," I say.

He frowns. "It is to me."

We hop onto our dirt bikes and ride to the Poxton landfill. The wind is nasty. To keep control of our bikes, we have to concentrate. Charlie loves the extra edge. He thinks the wind is something that can be defeated. He says, "This is the best night. This is unbelievable."

We hydroplane across puddles of motor oil.

Charlie's motorbike is green and black with bits of rust on the body. Cornpup used junkyard parts to build his own dirt bike. It's an ugly metal contraption, rusted from top to bottom, and the wheels aren't the right size, but it works. My bike is white and blue and silver, with thin tires and a shiny motor. It was on my front porch the day after Dad's funeral. Mom kept asking me if I stole it, which really pissed me off. I told her the truth: I had no idea where the dirt bike came from. It's still a mystery.

We ride along Two Mile Creek, cutting tracks in the mud and

hopping the knotted tree roots we call "demon fingers." We squeeze through a torn chain-link fence and maneuver between two parked semitrucks.

Charlie says, "Gas fumes are my favorite. They make me feel high."

I look back at Cornpup and shout, "Seriously! Can't you ride any faster?"

He shouts back at me, "I built this bike. It has personality. Your factory-made bikes have speed but no soul!"

"I don't understand half the stuff that comes out of his mouth," says Charlie. "I really don't."

Our wheels slip in the mud, but we don't wipe out. For Charlie and me, not being the first to fall is a matter of pride. Cornpup *has to* fall before we do, and then it's like a faucet has been turned on. We all fly off our bikes on purpose, laughing at each other. The more blood, the more mud, the better.

I look at Charlie and say, "Quick detour."

He nods, knowing exactly where I want to go, exactly where to turn.

Adjacent to our old elementary school is a landfill that first inspired me to draw. When I was really little, sitting on a swing, staring at broken cement slabs and PVC piping, I kept seeing faces of beasts in the rubble. Unlike Chemical Mountain, with its tall, dome-shaped peak and beautiful slopes, this landfill is a plateau, rugged and uncapped. It holds a collection of hazards—car batteries and computer monitors, deep holes and piles of slick fly ash, sludge that has hardened into oddly shaped boulders—and it feels like an obstacle course. At the far end of the landfill, there is a deep split in the earth, about four feet wide. We call it the fault line. Whenever I jump it, I always look down and wonder if it's a portal to another world, a place where creatures grow strong and evil, or if it's just a bunch of emptiness, an infinite hole.

"This used to drive me nuts when we were little," says Charlie.

"What's the point of putting a really fun landfill five feet away from a playground and then putting up a fence so we could look at the landfill all day but never play on it?"

"They didn't put the dump next to the school, you idiot," says Cornpup. "They built the school next to the dump. Because the land was cheap. That's what city commissioners do: they build schools on the cheapest land they can find, right next to some power lines, ten feet from an uncapped landfill, with weird smells outside so the teachers can't ever open the windows. And these politicians are so old, by the time we're eighteen and can *really* hold them accountable, they'll all be dead. Screwing over a bunch of kids is ingenious if you really think about it. We're the easiest targets."

"I'm so sick of your negativity," says Charlie. "If you hate it so much here, then move somewhere else."

"Both of you," I say. "Just shut up and ride." I try to peel away all cool like they do in the movies, but my bike does this sputtering thing that it's been doing lately, and I have to work the throttle for a few seconds before I get any decent pickup. Charlie accelerates past me. I watch him lift his face to the sky and howl like a wolf. Cornpup walks his bike over two large pieces of machinery. He stops to pick up something that looks like a round saw blade.

Me and Charlie race each other, neck and neck, adrenaline burning in our veins. I jump a propane tank and skid into a trench of black slime. Charlie rides up an aluminum ramp and jumps off the end. When Cornpup finally joins us, his nose is running.

"I found a Chinese star," he says.

I take off again, toward the far end of the landfill, my dirt bike moving at full speed. I dodge a methane vent at the last possible second. I fall into a pile of PVC pipes and wires. I watch Charlie ride with perfect balance along a thin steel beam. Cornpup is buzzing after us at a sorry pace. Me and Charlie stop and wait for him by a pile of rotting shingles.

126

Charlie strikes a match from his pocket and then drops it into a crater filled with a metallic liquid that makes me think of mercury. The flame explodes, jumping high above our heads, and my heart fills with a strange, peaceful feeling. How can Charlie create something like this, I wonder, with just one match? He always knows exactly how a thing will burn.

Cornpup isn't interested in the fire. He buzzes past us, like an old man on a scooter at the grocery store. Charlie rides off to join him, howling as he goes. My feet are planted on the ground. My bike idles quietly with an occasional sputter. I feel like I should do something about the fire, but I have no idea how to extinguish it. I sort of want to leave it burning, because it's beautiful, except maybe it will spread across the industrial fields, blackening everything like a total eclipse.

I watch Charlie slide his bike to a stop in Cornpup's path. I am sure a crash will follow, but Cornpup hits his breaks just in time. I watch them talk for a minute. I watch them laugh. I wonder why Cornpup is always so quick to forgive Charlie, who can be so mean. Or maybe it's Charlie who's forgiving Cornpup, for constantly pointing out the negative, for always being such a buzz kill.

"I'm almost out of gas!" Cornpup shouts to me.

I look at my own gauge, and it's low. I catch up with my friends, and park my bike next to Cornpup. I ask him what's wrong with his eye.

"A bug flew in it," he says.

Charlie's teeth are so white they almost glow in the dark, and this makes the spaces where his teeth are missing seem really obvious. He says, "I'm dying of hunger. When we get home, I'm gonna make myself a big old pot of macaroni and cheese."

Cornpup jumps the fault line first. I can't bear to watch. His dirt bike barely has enough power to lift off the ground, but he makes it up and over somehow. Me and Charlie go crazy cheering for him, laughing.

Charlie goes next. He borrows Cornpup's knit hat and pulls it down over his eyes. "I'm gonna jump this blindfolded," he says, and that's exactly what he does.

"Wow," says Cornpup. "That was stupid. And great."

I go last. I've jumped the fault line a hundred times, before Charlie even knew it was here. I'm not scared at all.

But when I take off, my back tire gets caught on a machine lever. One-tenth of a second is all it takes. My front tire makes it to the other side, spinning like a round saw into the dirt, and for a second I think I might live through this, until I feel the back half of my bike drop sharply down, a sudden dip that turns my stomach, my body sliding into the black canyon. I catch hold of a rock and grip it so tightly that my fingernails lift and bleed, and still my hands are slipping.

A dark part of me is whispering, *Let go of that rock. It feels good to fall. Stop fighting.* And memories start blinking through my mind like little bursts of light. I see Valerie bringing me a note on pink paper, Viper chewing a bone, me and Charlie and Cornpup running to the creek with our shoe boxes and jars. I see Randy on the porch steps teaching me guitar chords. I see Dad onstage at a festival by the river.

There is no adrenaline rush, no fear. I just feel . . . tired.

My right leg feels impossibly heavy. I think my dirt bike is caught on my jeans somehow, pulling me down. I wonder what I'm supposed to do about that.

I really do consider letting go. I think about falling to the center of the earth and never having to face freshman year or a fence around the creek, never having to fight Kevin Thompson, never having to be around all the people who secretly believe Dad deserved to die. I think about never again having to watch Mom wolfing down cheesecake. It would be so easy.

But I don't want to fall. I don't want this to be the end. I have things to live for. Charlie. Cornpup. Valerie. Viper. A sketchbook full of monsters. The Freak Tour. Revenge.

Two seconds have passed, maybe three, and I'm still thinking there might be a way to live, except I'm not strong enough to pull myself up. Never was. I take a deep breath of air, the way Charlie does, because I want to be a fighter like him, immortal. I breathe in the night smog, the gas fumes.

Charlie grabs my wrists. "I've got you," he says. His face is calm and focused. I don't think he even sees me right now. I think he sees fourth and twenty-seven, his team down by three, one second left on the clock. "And I've got your bike."

"What are you talking about?" Cornpup shouts. "He could *die*. Forget the bike!"

"No!" Charlie shouts. "I've got this."

He pulls me up with one arm. He pulls my bike up with the other. His strength is like an explosion. Suddenly I'm on the ground, safe and alive.

"Are you all right?" Cornpup asks me.

"Not really."

Charlie is running his hands along the body of my dirt bike, checking for scratches. It's like he cares about the bike more than anything else. "I don't see any major damage," he reports. "I don't see anything that can't be buffed out."

We ride toward home until Cornpup runs out of gas. Then we walk.

Charlie tells a funny story about our old PE teacher, who wears Windbreaker pants and farts when demonstrating how to do a proper sit-up. We snort with laughter. His observations about people are always so true. I love it when he turns on someone else. But I hate it when he turns on me.

Charlie used to rip on me a lot, used to say I had "girl arms." I actually tried to cut off our friendship because of it. I was done with him. He started calling my house every two seconds, throwing rocks at my window. "You *do* have girl arms," he said, "but I can help you. I can fix it." Eventually he wore me down. Three days later, we were friends again. He gave me his barbell and his jump rope. He taught me boot camp exercises. I'm still a lot skinnier than he is, a lot weaker, but my arms and back are cut, and my abs feel like a sheet of metal. It's hard to hate Charlie when you can see that he is making you stronger.

But it goes even deeper than that.

Charlie is honest. You always know where he stands. And he is generous. I'll hide my favorite movies so he won't ask to borrow them. I'll tell him I don't have any money because I don't want him to ask me to chip in for pizza when I'm not hungry. Then he'll lend me his new Bills T-shirt, before he's even had a chance to wear it, because he doesn't want me showing up at Valerie's pool party dressed in my stupid clothes, and I wonder who I'd be if Charlie wasn't here to influence me, to insult me, to toughen me up.

I would be a total loser without him. I would be an absolute nerd.

"We should go home," Cornpup says. "I feel like tonight's one of those nights when bad things are gonna just keep happening, and we should just cash it in. We can ride Chemical Mountain some other time, tomorrow even."

"This is what I mean about your endless negativity," says Charlie. "I saved his life. I saved the dirt bike. Couldn't that mean tonight is one of those nights when *good* things are gonna just keep happening?"

Cornpup looks at me.

"It's on the way home," I say. "It's not like we're going really far out of the way or anything."

At the base of Chemical Mountain, we are silent, offering up a prayer, I guess—*We come in peace, holy mountain. Don't kill us today*—except Cornpup is an atheist and would go off on us if we used the word *prayer*. I lose my breath every time I stand at the foot of this landfill. It towers over us, a steep incline with a deep, muddy base. The city has covered the slopes in stunning green sod and scattered patches of purple flowers, and even now, at close to midnight, the effect is beautiful. It feels like this isn't a landfill at all, like the chain-link fence and NO TRESPASSING signs were put here by mistake. But we know that's just not true. Cornpup says decorating a landfill is nothing but a public relations move. He says a group of people called "they" want this mountain to be beautiful so we forget what's inside. "People are retarded half the time," he always says. "They only remember stuff they see in commercials, and even then it can't be more than thirty seconds of information and there has to be a catchy little song."

"It always seems so much taller in person," I say. "Like in my memory I see a big hill, but in person, it's really a mountain. They should build ski lifts."

"I feel like it's alive," says Charlie. "Like it's growing. I want to be here the day it explodes."

We lug our bikes up the mountain. The view from the summit is breathtaking—lights from the Grand Island Bridge, gridlocked traffic on the 990, Two Mile Creek glistening in the moonlight, vast and empty industrial complexes. These things are all below us and feel so far away.

"Look down there." I point to an incinerator that's been boarded up since we were in fifth grade.

"So it's operational again," says Charlie. "So what?"

Cornpup laughs out loud. "It reopened between now and when we rode through here a few hours ago? *Not* likely."

I count the white vans. There are twelve. "I didn't know the incinerator still had power."

"They're using a generator," says Cornpup.

We coast down the dark side of the landfill, motors off, and stash our dirt bikes behind a steel drum at the edge of the railroad tracks. We creep closer to the incinerator. We can't take our eyes off the unmarked vans, the men in white coveralls, the spotlights and smoke. These men have waited until dark on purpose. We are witnessing a secret, something that shouldn't be happening.

"It looks like an invasion," I say.

"There's the ringleader." Cornpup points to a man wearing a black turtleneck and cargo pants. He is standing a hundred paces away from the incinerator and grips a walkie-talkie. He is looking out into the night, like a watchman, and none of the other men approach him.

I can barely choke out the words. "That's the guy from . . ."

"That night at the grain mill," says Charlie.

"The town meeting," says Cornpup.

Dad wasn't kidding when he told me Dan Benecke kept a close eye on every aspect of Mareno Chem operations. "He's everywhere," I say. "He's like a bad rash."

The incinerator is fired up like a carnival, with lights, movement, and a feeling of mystery.

Cornpup stands. "I'm gonna walk right up to that guy and ask him what they're doing."

"What?" I give him a weird look. "We're all muddy. I've got blood on my shirt. You're wearing *rubber gloves*, for chrissakes. We look stupid. You think we're going to intimidate these people?"

"I'll intimidate them," says Charlie.

Revenge. Maybe tonight's the night. Three of us against one.

Cornpup is already walking toward the lights.

CHAPTER 20
ANGER

SOMETHING about Cornpup charging through the muddy grass strikes me as the funniest thing I've ever seen. His hands are balled into fists. He's walking with his butt cheeks squeezed together. He has a leaf stuck to the back of his head. This confrontation—it is something he has wanted to do all his life. He has hated this landfill for such a long time. He has been angry at chemical companies and rogue polluters for such a long time. But Cornpup likes to fight by the rules. He uses words. He tries to reason with his opponent. Last time I checked, no war in the history of wars has ever been won with words.

Your enemies have to take you seriously. You need violence.

Cornpup knocks on Dan Benecke's back like he's knocking on a door. Dan Benecke turns around calmly. He sees me and Charlie first. Then he looks down at Cornpup, who waves. "Wow, kid," he says. "What are you supposed to be?"

I give Charlie a look. "Why didn't we at least force him to lose the dishwashing gloves?"

Cornpup points toward a row of houses at the edge of the industrial park. "I live over there."

I search Dan Benecke's face for a look of recognition. Does he remember us from the town meeting? Charlie questioning him about the chunky stuff in the creek. Cornpup showing off photographs and lumpy skin. Me, the quiet one, son of a dead man. Does he know I smashed up his office?

"Well," Dan Benecke says in his smooth, professional voice. "If you live over there, then that's where you should be right about now. This is private property. I'm sure you know how to read. I'm sure you know the definition of the word *trespassing*." He keeps his eyes on us as he brings the walkie-talkie up to his lips. "Take a five-minute break. I have company. Just some boys. I'll take care of it. Over."

"Take care of us how?" says Charlie.

Dan Benecke hooks his walkie-talkie onto his belt. "It's time for you kids to go on home."

Cornpup doesn't budge. "I think you should tell us what you're doing here."

The fake smile is gone. "Get out of here. I'm not asking."

"Your men," says Cornpup. "They're wearing hazmat gear. You're burning chemicals here. You're poisoning our neighborhood."

"Let's get something straight." Dan Benecke glares at us. "This is not a *neighborhood*. This is an industrial complex. You see those railcars over there? They're not playhouses. You see those metal drums? They're not picnic tables. You see that chain-link fence around the perimeter? It's not a decoration. You boys aren't supposed to be playing back here."

Interesting choice of words, *playing*. He thinks we're little kids. He's not scared of us.

"Dumping at night," says Cornpup. "You aren't supposed to be playing back here either."

Dan Benecke doesn't fit my typical villain profile. He is not an ice monster. He's not a creek serpent. He is strong, self-assured, a little bit like Charlie, but without the blood and bruises. When he puts his hand on Cornpup's back and starts escorting us off the premises, I almost feel like he's protecting us.

"Get your hands off me." Cornpup whips around. "I said I'd bring your whole company down, and I meant it. But especially you. I want to ruin you personally, because you're the one signing off on all this. You think because you're rich you can get away with things, but you should've watched out for me. I've got nothing to lose."

It's funny how we all hate this guy, but for different reasons. Cornpup wants the dumping to stop. He thinks Mareno Chem is out to poison us all. Charlie doesn't care about the dumping; he just wants it to be less obvious. He's pissed that Mareno Chem has done things to draw attention to our creek, our *territory*. I hate this man because he reached inside my family and took Dad away from me. He took Mom away from me too, if I really stop and think about it.

"You need to leave. Now, or I'm calling the police." Dan Benecke's lip is twitching so wildly, I want to reach out and touch it, make it stop.

Cornpup smirks. "I dare you to call the police. When they see what you're dumping here, they won't arrest us. They'll arrest *you*."

I'm not sure that's true. Mareno Chem owns this town. I bet every cop in Poxton has at least one family member working in the chemical manufacturing plant.

Dan Benecke holds up his flashlight, like he wants to beat us, like we're dogs. He had that same look on his face when he scared

Mom into signing a stack of legal papers. If I don't hurt him now, I'll regret it for the rest of my life.

The Chinese star Cornpup found at the dump is so sharp, it's cutting through his back pocket. I grab the circular weapon, and it burns in my hand.

"Oh, man. What are you gonna do with that?" says Charlie.

"Give it back to me," says Cornpup. "Don't be stupid."

I don't think Dan Benecke understands what a Chinese star even is, because he's looking at me strangely, when what he really should be doing is running away in a zigzag pattern. I will cut up Dan Benecke's face. I will shred his skin until he looks like the monster that he is. I want him to hurt like I hurt. And I want him to live with hideous scars for as long as I have to live without Dad.

"Jason, man, whatever you're thinking about doing, he's not worth it," Charlie says in a low voice.

Tears are running down my cheeks. "You guys won't rat me out. I can cut his face. I can cut out his eyeballs. No one will know it was me."

"This isn't you," says Cornpup. "Your dad wouldn't want this."

My hands are shaking. I just need to make the first cut. From there, it will be easy.

Dan Benecke grabs Cornpup's arm and twists it back violently. I try to think where I've heard a bone pop like that before. If this guy was scared of me, he'd be running away. Instead, he is getting ready to break Cornpup's arm.

He is daring me to cut him. His eyes have gone all empty. He doesn't hear Cornpup's asthma kicking in, thick wheezing sounds that make you want to cry. He doesn't respond when Charlie shouts, "Let him go, mister. Seriously. What are you trying to do? Just let him go."

"He's gonna have an asthma attack," I say. "He needs his inhaler or he'll die."

Still no reaction.

Cornpup's wheezing gets worse.

There is a sharp weapon in my hand. I need to use it.

Charlie tries to pry Cornpup free. Dan Benecke's elbow flies up at a sharp angle. He knocks Charlie in the jaw. I hear the sick sound of bone on bone. Charlie falls backward into the bubbling mud. I hear the sound of uncontrolled wheezing, a windpipe closing. Dan Benecke tosses Cornpup to the ground like he's not even a person, like he's a product, a bag of cat food.

I reach out and cut Dan Benecke's cheek. Just once, to show him how unlucky he could've been tonight. Then I throw the Chinese star to the ground. Cornpup was right. Dad wouldn't want this. I have to walk away.

"I remember your father," Dan Benecke says, running his fingers along his wound, studying the blood. "He was average in every way. He could've worked at Mareno Chem for thirty years, blending in with all the other empty faces. But no, he had to open his big mouth. While we were fine-tuning Phenzorbiflux, hoping to reapply for EPA approval, he was stealing information from our computers, gathering data that could've opened us up to a lot of lawsuits. When he died, I thought, *How sad.* If he'd been paying attention to his safety gear instead of sticking his nose where it didn't belong, he might've had a long, simple life. I wouldn't say he was a smart man."

I jump on Dan Benecke with such force he falls to the ground. I punch him in the face again and again and again. I'll never stop punching this man. I'll stay here forever.

Cornpup manages to squirm away.

I feel hands on my shoulders. "You got him good," Charlie says. "Let's go."

I don't want to look at Dan Benecke's face, but I can't help it. I have to know if I've hurt him. For a sliver of a second I lock eyes with this man. I fully expect him to jab his fist into my face, but he doesn't. He is wearing an expression I've never seen on anyone before. Maybe he is ashamed the situation escalated to this level. Maybe he is stunned.

Or maybe he seriously wants to kill me.

We take off running. We go straight for the fence. We don't pass the water pump. We don't collect our dirt bikes. We don't look back. The sound of our hands hitting the chain-link fence is the only sound that matters. We climb up and over.

Charlie licks the fresh blood from his lips. "Jason. I don't know what that was, but you rule."

My knuckles are throbbing. I feel like a uranium monster, hot and indestructible. I also feel a little bit sad inside. Revenge didn't fix the parts of me that are broken.

I wonder if I took things too far. When Charlie has to pull you off someone, you've gone too far.

"You stopped at one cut," says Cornpup. "It could've been worse."

"Worse?" says Charlie. "You're the one who keeps telling us that innocent people are dying because Mareno Chem is dumping toxic waste all over the place. That guy destroyed Jason's family. He deserved a hell of a lot worse than a tiny cut and some gut punches."

The cut wasn't tiny. It was shallow, yes, but it took up the whole side of his face. I'm scared of how close I came to really shredding him.

My friends slap me on the back. They're laughing.

We walk past the S&R pipe factory. Cornpup tells us the workers put so much mercury in the ground the trees turned silver for a while. I don't think that's true. We walk past the old Spaulding Fibre plant. Cornpup points to its demolished silo and says there are PCBs buried four feet below the surface. I have no idea what PCBs are, nor do I care.

I tell Cornpup all about my Freak Tour idea, and he is pumped.

Charlie is quiet. I can feel him watching me. Machines are pounding in my head. Maybe he can hear them.

CHAPTER 21
FREAK TOUR

WE spend all of the next night working on our Freak Tour. We want it to be legendary and perfect. We want to get this right. At ten-thirty, Mom falls asleep on the couch, hugging a jar of peanut butter like it's a kitten. I take the spoon out of her hand and put a blanket on her. "There's an earthquake in the freezer," she murmurs.

We sneak out of a window in the den, Cornpup cutting his hand somehow, and Charlie nearly kicking the TV off its stand with his huge feet. It's like he's just too big for this world, too noisy. I glance over my shoulder at the door of the den. If Mom wakes up and finds a window propped open with a cinder block from the garage; Charlie's legs flailing, his body halfway outside the window; and our coffee table all covered in mud from Cornpup's boots, then I'll be in deep trouble.

Cornpup is wearing rubber boots that come to his knees. Charlie has a long, heavy black flashlight he found at the army surplus store. I sketch ideas in a notebook as we walk. I draw a snake with rusty metal scales and two long screws for fangs. I draw an exhaust creature with a muffler head and rusty tailpipe limbs.

"I wish I could draw like that," Charlie says as we cut across the mudflats.

I feel suddenly proud, even a little arrogant. He'll never know what it's like to create monsters. This talent is all mine.

Viper likes to be out at night. His ears move at every sound: screeching owls, buzzing streetlights, chirping frogs. I can hear his wet nose *sniff-sniffing*. It's crazy, how happy dogs are sometimes, how content.

Tonight we're walking the tour route, a practice run before the real deal. We're on high alert, our eyes ready to pick out hazards and delays. There's a short argument about where to start the tour, even though we all know it should probably start at Cornpup's house. I've got the nosy neighbors who report things to my mom. It's hard enough hiding Viper from them.

"My house, then," says Charlie. He lights matches as we walk. It's like he's been craving fires lately. I close my eyes and think of silver mercury demons, slithering out of the ground, latching on to our ankles like vines. Charlie would fight them all with a matchbook and some gasoline. He has to be the center of attention always.

"Your house? Are you kidding?" Cornpup snorts.

We can't risk having his drunk dad around.

And so we're back at Cornpup's house, which is where we should've started. His backyard dead-ends at a torn chain-link fence, the obvious portal to our world of buried sludge and dark machines. It's just that Cornpup also has the worst of all possible things—a stay-at-home mom. She will not be cool with a bunch of noisy kids in her yard, and if she sees us slip through that fence, she'll call the cops for sure. She's that dramatic.

"We'd have to start the tour at exactly ten Saturday morning and get back no later than twelve," Cornpup says. "She'll be at the salon getting a manicure, even though I need new shoes and Abbi needs glasses. She's so freaking selfish."

Mom once said, "Courtney Schumacher would let her sump pump go out before she'd cancel the weekly pedicure. How am I supposed to keep up with all that beauty, all that *irresponsibility?*" I wanted to tell her she was no better, that sometimes it felt like she'd sell me into slavery for a pan of meatloaf, but I kept my mouth shut.

"If I calculated this right, we've got five minutes at each stop." Cornpup is messing with the stopwatch he dropped into the toilet a few nights ago. He was trying to set a record for longest piss. He said it was one of those awkward moments when you have to decide what's worse, sticking your hand in your own pee or flushing the toilet and clogging a pipe with an object that can be traced back to you. He put his hand in the pee. The stopwatch still works.

"Five minutes is doable," I say.

"Cornpup, you're stressing me out," says Charlie. "We'll be back on time. I promise you. Even if I have to rescue a bunch of kids from the quicksand pit, *we will be back on time.*"

He's not talking about real quicksand. He's talking about a gurgling pit of leaves and mud that never seems to dry. He's talking about how we once put a metal yardstick into the pit, only to discover that the pit was much deeper than we thought. The yardstick never did touch bottom, and when we pulled it out, it looked like it had been partially digested.

"Lucky we didn't stick our fingers in there," Cornpup said.

"I'm not scared. I'll stick my hand in there," Charlie said. But he didn't do it.

I think about the fire we started later that night, how wrong it all went. The trees were dead in the first place—we didn't kill them—but to see all those branches burning was real creepy. There were sparks flying everywhere, and some of those sparks turned into miniature fires that had to be dealt with. Cornpup worked on extinguishing the original bonfire that was raging like crazy. Charlie chased the flying sparks and stomped out the small fires, even though his throwing hand was bleeding and he was in pain. I was in charge of the trees, but without a hose, what was I really supposed to do? I poured creek water and sand at the base of the trees, and then I just allowed them to burn out. I was scared that night, and Cornpup was annoyed, but Charlie was thrilled. I think there was a part of him that wanted to have burn marks on his skin. He probably would jump into the quicksand and save some kid. I can picture him screaming and melting, his muscles visible where his skin gets eaten away, his peacock-blue eyes bulging from his face. I really don't think he'd hesitate. I think he'd want to be a hero, eaten alive in a pit of acid.

I keep thinking about last night, what I did to Dan Benecke's face. I got my revenge. It should be over. But it's not over. He will strike back.

The industrial park is creepy tonight. Most of the lights are either dim or flickering, they're so poorly maintained. There are dead trees with gnarled bare branches that look like cracks in the glassy sky. There are steel containers that leak clear, steamy liquid into the soil. We hear bats in the tall brick silos. Dump trucks sleep like animals near high piles of mysterious sludge. An ammonia tanker without wheels is lying on its side in a patch of tall grasses that hiss when the wind blows. I get the feeling anything could happen here.

We walk along a trail of deep, glossy puddles, bright green water during the day and deep forest-green water at night. Cornpup doesn't step in these puddles, because to him they're dangerous chemical landmines. I don't step in the puddles because I have to keep my shoes looking clean and new for as long as possible; Mom won't take me shopping till my toes pop out, and even then it's a battle. Charlie, though, he steps in the puddles. He tries to splash us.

I ask Cornpup about the detox teas and the special skin creams. "Are you sure you really need to buy all that stuff?"

"Dr. Gupta can remove my cysts, but I'll still have scars and rashes. Plus, my body can't filter out toxins in a normal way. Herbal supplements should help. If you're asking me 'Am I sure it will work?' the answer is, 'I have no idea.' But I feel like this is my last chance. I have to at least try."

I nod like I understand, but I don't. I've been in the creek more than he has, and Charlie pretty much lives in that water. My skin is smooth and perfect. Charlie's body is healthy and strong.

Cornpup is a guy like us, but he's saying he's made of something different. Skin cells that aren't working? Weak organs? Poor blood? And it's all just a product of bad genes? Bad luck?

We don't learn about these things in school. We don't learn about these things anywhere.

Charlie grabs Viper's leash from my hand and walks ahead of us, out of earshot. I don't want him out there in the darkness with my dog. I think of all the things he won't notice—snakes and broken glass and skunks and syringes. I want to tell him to come back, but he'd take that as a dare to walk farther out of sight.

"And you trust this doctor? You really trust him? You're sure he's not scamming you?"

Cornpup looks at me. "He's legit. I called the hospital and checked him out. The surgery is free."

"But you always say *nothing* is free," I argue. "You're the one who always says to watch for ulterior motives."

Cornpup's not mad at me, but I can see he's frustrated—at himself, maybe, for not explaining this right. He is exhausted all the time. "Jason, you're just gonna have to back off. I asked the right questions. Dr. Gupta was open with me. He does get something out of this deal. He needs more data on chemical sensitivities in people under eighteen. I'll be part of his research. One day he'll probably use my 'before' and 'after' pictures to generate new business. I'm okay with that."

"So you're an experiment?"

"You can't tell me that's worse than being a cyst-covered freak. You don't know how it feels. You and Charlie *can't even imagine* how it feels. I will always back you, no matter what. Right now, I need you to do the same for me."

I get the message loud and clear. Earlier today, Cornpup surprised me by offering way more help with the Freak Tour than I was expecting. He gave me a box of expensive calligraphy pens he'd found in Gramps's desk. He spoke to a librarian friend of his, and she told him there's a way to print double-sided pages, and *of course* I can use the library's copy machines for free. Then, at the pawnshop, he found a bookbinding machine that uses hot glue to make the bindings. I don't know what he traded to get it, but the contraption is sitting on my bedroom floor, and it's mine forever, he says. *Forever*.

Cornpup wants a shot at having normal skin forever. Even if it makes me uncomfortable knowing he's gonna be part of some plastic surgeon's research, I have to let it go. I have to let him do his thing.

When we catch up to Charlie, he's scheming up ways to sell Freak Tour tickets. "First I spread the word, get all the kids buzzing. Then I create the illusion of limited ticket supply. After that, we lock them into a bidding war."

I have no idea what Charlie's talking about. We're selling the tickets for a set price, and no eight-year-old is going to start a bidding war.

"He scalped three Bills tickets in front of the Big Tree Inn last season, and now he thinks he's some kind of marketing genius," says Cornpup.

On the day of the tour, Charlie will be my bouncer. He says he'll confiscate cameras and hit kids with a stick if they complain about being thirsty or needing to use the bathroom. If it comes down to it, he'll handcuff disruptive kids with zip ties to "set an example."

I tell him I can see this spiraling out of control. Then we all bust out laughing.

We talk about what Cornpup's role will be on the day of the tour. He wants to be a secretary or something. He'll collect tickets, sell my books, and keep track of the money. He'll grill each of the children and make sure none of their leaky mouths ratted us out to any parents—or worse, to the cops. My only job is to tell horrible stories, to make children feel fear, to breathe life into dead chemical sites. It seems easy, but the thought of talking for two solid hours freaks me out. Maybe they will hate my stories. Maybe I won't be able to keep their attention. Maybe this whole thing is a mistake.

"See that?" Cornpup points to a massive cement drainage pipe behind a dimly lit building within the Mareno Chem complex. The pipe is barfing up dark, chunky sludge. The smell is a mix of burnt plastic and nail polish remover. "They're still dumping. They never stopped."

We sit on the banks of Two Mile Creek for a long time, coughing till our lungs burn. Charlie plays a drumbeat on the ground with two sticks. Cornpup watches the drainage pipes, his eyes willing the sludge to stop, except there seems to be no end to it. Viper sniffs for lizards and mice. I lie back in the dirt and look up at the stars. I wonder if Dad can see me—an unoriginal thought, I know. I'll bet every kid with a dead parent wonders what I wonder. We all talk in our heads to someone who won't ever answer.

Later, me and my friends will walk home. We'll fall asleep before the first rays of morning sun, before our parents start brewing instant coffee and spitting phlegm into the sink and frying eggs in corn oil. Before Randy rides his motorcycle to Molly's house. Before

Abbi pounds her little hands on the kitchen table and chants, *Pancakes! Pancakes!* Before the drainage pipes go silent and the creek moves, all dark and dirty, over golf balls, beer cans, and shiny rocks.

Tomorrow we won't see each other. I'll write out my stories, and Charlie will sell tickets, and I don't know what Cornpup will do. Maybe he'll be meeting with the doctor, prepping his skin for the big surgery.

Earlier this morning, I saw Kevin Thompson at the junkyard. I was looking for an antenna for Mom, and he was carrying a steering wheel. I saw him eyeing me, and there were all these weapons he could've grabbed—rusty sheets of metal, jagged exhaust pipes, long shards of broken glass—but he didn't say or do anything. I hope that's a sign of what's to come, that if I see him in the hallway freshman year, he'll just walk on by, like a total stranger. It's funny how I used to be so scared of him.

What I'm scared of now is harder to pinpoint. I'm scared I could lose my friend to an experimental surgery. I'm scared of telling my landfill stories to a bunch of little kids. I'm scared Dan Benecke will do something terrible to me and Mom. But most of all, I'm scared of this feeling I have deep down in my bones. It's the same restless feeling I had the night Dad didn't come home. I feel like something in my life is about to shift in a horrible way.

CHAPTER 22
LANDFILL MYTHOLOGY

I should've known something would go wrong. On Thursday morning, Mareno Chem put a notice in the paper, something about how parents need to keep their teenagers from trespassing in the industrial yards. It could mean they're gonna be patrolling our tour route. Then, on Friday night, Gramps had chest pains. He drove himself to the hospital with maple syrup on his gas pedal. It was a heart attack. No one bothers to tell Cornpup till Saturday, about thirty minutes before the Freak Tour is set to begin.

"What do you mean, you're not coming?" Charlie is sitting at my kitchen table, shoveling spoonfuls of Cinnamon Toast Crunch into his mouth, spilling milk all over Mom's new place mats, and shouting into the phone.

"He's not coming?" I say.

Charlie slams the phone down so hard I expect to see an explosion of wires and little electrical components. "Unbelievable."

I should care about Gramps. I should care that Cornpup is worried about his only living grandfather. *I should care. I should care. I should care.* But I don't. All this work for nothing, my hand aching from hours of calligraphy pens, the time it took for me to finally feel proud of my book.

"Maybe no one was gonna show up anyway." I put my glass in the sink.

Charlie looks at me. "We're not canceling anything. We can meet him at the hospital later."

It's supposed to be all three of us doing this thing. How many times have I gone with Cornpup to the library or the pawnshop, always running errands with him, when what I really wanted to do was race my dirt bike on an open road? Me and Charlie sat through a long, stupid town meeting about Two Mile Creek, even though we had better places to be. We back each other up. That's how it is. That's how it's always been.

Charlie doesn't care about glitches in our master plan. He says, "We're doing this thing. We're gonna rock the tour and make a lot of money."

At quarter to ten the Schumachers' yard is swarming with neighborhood kids and their friends. I was worried a few parents would show up, but that hasn't happened. I was waiting for a squad car to drive by, but that hasn't happened either. There are thirty-two little nerds in all, and so far no one has tried to pay in pennies.

Charlie has been *weird* today. He gave me his lockbox and told me not to open it till he's famous. "Just put it under your bed," he said. "And then forget it's there." Then he made me leave Viper at home with a gigantic rawhide bone, and even though Mom won't be home from work till around dinnertime, I still feel anxious. Now he has the kids standing shoulder to shoulder behind the

Schumachers' garage while he picks a large scab off his knee too early, his eyes studying the bright new blood.

"Are you nervous or something?" I ask him.

"No." He answers slowly, like he is confused by the question. "I don't get nervous."

Then I ask Charlie how much money we have, and he pats the bulge in the front pocket of his jeans as if to say, *Plenty. I'll keep it safe. Don't worry.* We might have a lot of money, because all but two of my books have sold, and it bothers me that Charlie won't say a number out loud. I think of him skimming off the top, or worse, losing it all, the way he "lost" my margarine tub full of cash so many years ago.

Charlie is wearing plastic gloves and tall rubber boots. He paces back and forth with his hands clasped behind his back. He barks rules at the kids, "No talking, or you're off the tour. We don't give second chances. We don't give refunds."

The kids are quiet around us, cautious. We've never really even spoken to them before. I think Charlie's gloves are scaring them. When the nurse is doing a lice check at school, I don't care about the black plastic combs. It's the gloved hands I worry about. I know how dirty my house can get when Mom is working lots of doubles, and I think, *Please not me. Please don't let me be the lice kid.* And it never is me. I've never had bugs in my hair. But I know what it feels like to see gloves on the hands of a person who is not your friend, to feel like you're gonna puke when you smell latex.

"Follow Charlie," I say. My voice comes out shaky. I'm not used to an audience, even if it is a mob of local children. I should know each of their names—Poxton is a small town, after all—but I've always kept my attention on the older crowd, Randy and his friends. I'm interested in people who have motorcycles and garage bands and who actually do stuff with their lives.

To save time, we skip the introductions. I make up my own names for the kids. There is Squinty Boy, and Girl in Turtle Sweatshirt, and Cat Eyes, and Stupid Shoes. There is Snot Nose, and Knee Pads, and Stick Arms, and Long-Hair Girl. There is Gap Tooth, and Apricot Ears, and Horse T-shirt, and Band-Aid Knee. I name all thirty-two kids in this way, my eyes snagging on one feature. I wonder what me and my friends would be called if we were judged so quickly. Cyst Boy? Fat Lady's Son? Fire Starter?

The kids squeeze through the torn chain-link fence and fan out into the industrial park.

Charlie tries with one hand to rip a rusty NO TRESPASSING sign off its hook, but the sign is secure, and he gets a brownish-red sliver of metal stuck in the tip of his thumb. If Cornpup were here, he'd be saying, *Tetanus shot. Your jaw is gonna lock up. Emergency room.* If Viper were here, he'd be sniffing the dead bird rotting at the base of the fence.

We trek across the field, a gray and windowless building looming up ahead, deep pockets of wet earth sucking at our shoes. When the puddles turn green and glossy, I start my first story.

"Aliens landed here," I say. "They were tall, like cement silos. They had claw arms for eating multiple children, shish kebab–style. They wore steel masks with radio receivers built in, night vision. Their spaceship was all busted-up and smoky. They spoke a strange language, grunts and whistles. Their weapons were like nothing you've ever seen. Metallic shapes, blinding lights."

I show an illustration from my book. The kids are mesmerized.

"They have lots of weapons," says Stupid Shoes.

Charlie stirs the green puddles with a stick. He says, "The aliens were injured in the crash. This is their blood. If you touch it, your skin will melt off."

The kids lean over the giant puddles. Charlie splashes the green liquid at them, and they jump back, horrified. It would be so funny if one of them fell in.

We walk the length of the industrial park, along rows of parked semitrucks and dark buildings, closed for the weekend. The whole area is hauntingly abandoned, like a mining town built on worthless soil. Seagulls soar overhead.

At the quarry I talk about crazy scientists. Trapdoors. An experiment gone bad. Bombs powered by lightning. Spies and an underground explosion.

At the dead black trees, I talk about the garlic fields burning, vampires climbing to the highest branches, their faces hidden in old gas masks. Screaming bats. Deep, gray smoke that twirled in violent spirals to the sky.

At the quicksand pit, I speak of Chemical War II. Smelly creatures rising up from the muck. A fog of ammonia and chlorine. Witch doctors running along the bubbly ground, their boots melting, their spells failing. Ashes and petroleum.

We walk to the tool and die plant, where baby dragon skeletons can be found. I tell the kids, "Never go near dragon bones without a sword for protection. Some dragon skeletons go on living without hearts or lungs, and they breathe an invisible fire that burns like the surface of the sun."

Midway through the tour, Charlie spots two cop cars and some security trucks driving really slowly through the industrial yards. We hide behind some leaky barrels, my heart pounding in my chest. I don't know if they're just cruising, looking for trespassers, or if they got tipped off that we're here, and they're looking for us. Long-Hair Girl touches something she's not supposed to and gets chemical burns on her hands. Charlie tells her to put mud on them. When the cops and security guards finally disappear, we all try to pretend we never saw them to begin with.

We pass the rubber factory where Joe Farley died. I tell the kids, "He didn't exactly fall. The real truth is that he got pulled down from the window by ghosts. There were claw marks all over his arms. Certain ghosts enjoy eating splattered brains. He's a ghost now too." As I say this, I feel guilty. Am I crossing some kind of line? Is it disrespectful to bring a real dead kid into my story?

We enter an old chemical plant, where I talk about pods of giant insects that buzz like generators. Behind the tanks, a praying mantis the size of a delivery truck is hissing at us. In the empty administrative office, I point to ants bigger than wolves, earthworms that look like anacondas, termites that eat flesh, black flies that puke rivers of poison when they land, cockroaches that could crush a minivan.

"If you go in here without our protection, you better bring a can of Raid and a prayer," says Charlie.

We enter the steel mill where huge killer rats move in large packs, their rapid footsteps causing small earthquakes. "Their matted gray fur is riddled with maggots. They sharpen their teeth on the blast furnace hinges. They're immune to rat poison. The rat leader has long fangs and a severed tail. He rigged this building with a million traps. You can set some of them off with stones, but if you step in the wrong place, they will catch you. They love to eat children who scream. They'll chill your blood and drink it like iced tea. That's just the way it is."

Charlie disappears into the darkness. He waits till a silent moment and then kicks an aluminum can across the floor. The sound of hollow metal rolling on sawdust is just like the sound of a massive rat attack, and the kids clear out of the mill, terrified. Cat Eyes is crying. Squinty Boy might've peed his pants. Long-Hair Girl's eyes are big and blue with horror.

"No crying," I tell them.

At the creek, I notice the sludge has thickened. The air smells like wet cement and paint thinner. The drainage pipes leading from Mareno Chem are silent, resting in the daylight. Tonight, they will be barfing up sludge again.

"You think these are just knotted tree roots," I say, "but you're wrong. You're looking at real demon fingers that'll grab you and drag you down to a world full of blood rivers and welded steel tor-ture devices. Screaming red ravens; billions of ants with ether-laced feet; monsters made of salt; crabs with razor-blade claws; hot mer-cury dripping from the sky."

I think about Viper. Is he done with the rawhide? Is he lonely all alone in my room?

A bird with sludge on its wings writhes around, trying to clean its feathers, but the sludge will dry heavy, like cooling metal. The bird can't fly, which means a fox will eat it.

"The creek water changes color," I tell the kids. "Green is alien blood. Red is goblin pee. Black sludge is demon diarrhea. Rainbow sheens are creek monster saliva. Chunky water has goblin snot in it. A strong chemical smell means your flesh will disintegrate if you swim. Black slime in the water has something to do with blind, poisonous snakes."

I don't know how we're doing on time. Charlie forgot to start the stopwatch. I feel like we've been walking for hours.

At the field of barrels, I talk about robot battles, metal pieces fly-ing everywhere, dark machines with bombs. I am tempted to show the kids Cornpup's robot, but I don't want them to know where we buried it.

At the tracks, Charlie lifts kids into the railcars, where we smash phosphorus rocks until we get sick of watching sparks fly.

At the pond by the incinerator, I point out the dead frogs and a tumor fish, how the water will sometimes steam, all signs that the landfill nymphs will soon return, with long coils of copper wires for hair, their eyes pure gray like an April sky.

We pass the place where Cornpup found the Chinese star, and where white unmarked vans invaded the incinerator on the night I almost died at the fault line. I clasp and unclasp my fists. I still remember how it felt, my knuckles against Dan Benecke's gut. Raw, uncontrollable rage.

We stop at the cold patch of ground. It's a dead zone. Not even insects and snakes go here. It's a hot summer morning, and we're freezing. Knee Pads and Stupid Shoes roll around on the cool mud. Girl in Turtle Sweatshirt and Cat Eyes hug themselves to stay warm. I wonder what's buried here, what could possibly make our breath turn smoky white months before the first freeze.

"Violent ice monsters live here in underground villages. They are wart-covered and carnivorous, obese but quick-moving, balding and oily. Sometimes they surface, causing sudden ice storms and a severe drop in temperature."

Charlie picks up a rock. He throws it over the tracks. It lands with a splash in the pond by the incinerator. A throw that distance shouldn't even be possible. He has a golden arm, talent he barely even understands. The kids cheer, and I'm pissed off at him for stealing the attention, but when I look at the kids' faces—Squinty Boy with his big glasses, Long-Hair Girl with a Blow Pop in her mouth, Band-Aid Knee with blood dripping down his leg—I see they're not watching Charlie anymore.

They've gone back to watching me.

Squinty Boy says, "I want to hear about the giant insect warrior who shoots beetles from a golden slingshot in the woods at the other side of the tracks."

Band-Aid Knee says, "Take us to the footprint by the power lines, the one that belongs to a creepy guy from the abusive traveling circus. Does he really cook squirrels and rats on an open grill? Does he really pick his teeth with twigs?"

We make one last stop, at Chemical Mountain, where I talk about the uranium monster. I give him rough, burnt skin. I give him wicked eyes. I tell them he eats radioactive candy bars. I tell them he lives in the landfill's belly, and that he takes a long whizz in our drinking water sometimes.

The kids laugh at this, even though I wasn't really trying to be funny.

At the end of the tour, they clap for me like I'm a movie star.

It almost hurts when we come up on Cornpup's house, when we slip through the fence that separates this land of legends from our regular lives. I don't want to stop telling stories.

"Good. Mrs. Schumacher's not back yet," says Charlie.

We watch the kids swarm the sidewalks. Squinty Boy has my book tucked into his back pocket. Girl in Turtle Sweatshirt looks back at us and waves. I thought I'd want to take a nap after the tour. I thought I'd feel wiped out and empty. Instead, I feel amped up with energy. I couldn't sleep now for anything.

We walk down Cardinal Drive. We pass old houses, old cars. I can't wait till later tonight. I'm gonna tap on Val's window at midnight. I'm gonna get her to sneak out and come with me to the creek. We'll take Viper for a long walk. We'll go swimming in the dark. It's gonna be awesome.

"So how much money did we make?" I look Charlie in the eye, so he can't bullshit me.

"Hundred and fifty bucks," he says. "And I know how we can make even more."

"Maybe we've done enough," I tell him. "Maybe Cornpup can come up with the rest of the money himself."

"No. Just listen. We sell tickets for a campout on the banks of Two Mile. Scary stories around the campfire. We can get Molly and Randy to chaperone. We can sell little bags of chips, cans of soda."

I give him a skeptical look. "I don't know. A whole entire night with those kids could be annoying."

Charlie laughs. "It'll be great. It'll be cool." He pauses. "Why is your mom's van in the driveway? I thought she had to work today."

My heart beats so fast I think it might detonate. I think even Charlie is afraid now. Because this is serious. She found Viper. I already know it. I can already feel it.

CHAPTER 23
HEAVY

WHEN we were ten, me and Charlie got trapped in a wrecked car at the junkyard. We climbed inside—Charlie in the driver's seat, me riding shotgun—and it never occurred to us that getting out would be a problem. It was a hot summer day, and we pretended we were cruising on an open highway, nothing but grazing cows and cherry orchards for miles and miles. Then the sun started heating the car's interior the way a gas flame heats a saucepan, and I said to Charlie, "This is not good." He made popping, sizzling sounds with his mouth, like he was an egg frying, but I didn't laugh. The passenger and driver's side doors were smashed up and wouldn't open. We were able to partially roll down one of the windows, but we couldn't squeeze through. A junkyard employee came to rescue us. He was a limping ogrelike guy who looked exactly—down to the harelip and gnarled fingers and blue veins—like a monster I'd drawn earlier that same day. Charlie noticed it too. He said, "That guy is your sewer goblin. That guy is not supposed to exist."

Years later, on a cold January morning, I had to help carry Dad's coffin. I felt confused, like the funeral couldn't possibly be real. I was still looking forward to our Sunday night ritual, me and Dad cooking minestrone together while Mom bleached her mustache in the bathroom. I remember Charlie saying, "Your dad can't be dead. I just saw him eating chicken wings three days ago."

So it's not like I don't know how it feels when unexpected things happen.

We walk into my kitchen and catch Mom eating a salad. Her hand freezes midbite, a forkful of romaine lettuce stopping one inch from her lips. There are tomato seeds on the cutting board. I see splashes of red and pale green and orange and purple—tomatoes and celery and carrots and salad onions. Certain things are *missing*. I don't see a slab of chuck steak or a frozen pizza. I don't see two slices of pie or a box of cinnamon rolls. I don't see greasy napkins or an empty liter of pop or a crumpled-up bag of potato chips in the garbage. The table is empty except for the salad and one tall glass of water with ice cubes in it.

Charlie says, "This is a little strange."

Viper is under the kitchen table chewing a squeaky toy I didn't buy him. His tail thumps on the linoleum when he sees me. His bowls have been moved over by the refrigerator. I notice fresh water in one, a real bone and shreds of meat in the other.

"You gave him tenderloin?" I say lamely.

Mom takes another bite and says, "No matter how hard I try, I can't get used to the feel of leaves in my mouth."

I reach out and touch the wall, because my legs feel bendy like spark plug wires. Seeing Mom in front of a plate of greens is like seeing Charlie in a ballerina skirt—*impossible*. And what does it mean that she fed good cuts of meat to my dog? Is she welcoming Viper to the family, telling him he can stay? Or is this like his Last Supper before she dumps him at the kill shelter?

Mom stabs a tomato chunk with her fork. Without looking up she says, "Charlie, go home."

She is never friendly to him, but today there is something else—agitation, understanding, indifference—I can't even tell anymore. She caught him spray painting his name on the street last weekend. She took the spray canister away from him and threw it down a nearby storm sewer, which is probably illegal, but whatever.

Charlie opens his eyes real wide and gives me a *Good luck, you're gonna need it* smile. He lets the screen door slam when he leaves, and Mom winces at the sound.

I hear too much breathing, too much chewing, not enough words.

The pile of groceries on the counter makes me think of Dad, how he used to cook the best meals. I'm not sure Mom even knows what to do with garlic bulbs, boneless chicken breasts, whole wheat pasta, and baby portobellos, but Dad taught me some stuff, so I can teach her. I remember exactly how much basil he used in his sauce.

Mom wears her factory uniform like a man—sweaty armpits, heavy boots, and a roll of fat over the belt. I once saw her clipping her toenails at the table. She blows her nose a lot, mostly at night, and it sounds like a semitruck honking. Now she's holding her fork all ladylike, and it's freaking me out.

I hear the clock ticking, canine jaws working at a chew toy, the washing machine squealing through a spin cycle. I notice a buzzing black fly that is trapped between our kitchen window and the screen.

"I found a dog in your room," she finally says.

"Did you get fired?" I ask her.

She shakes her head.

"Then why are you home early?"

Mom closes her eyes. "There was a bad accident at the plant. A woman—my friend—was injured. She's in the hospital."

"Which friend?" I demand without sympathy.

"Jeannie."

I know *exactly* who she's talking about. They eat at country buffets together.

"Tell me why there's a dog in my house," Mom says in a weary voice. I do things that make her feel exhausted, and she wants me to know it.

"I'm keeping him."

Mom takes another bite of green leaves. Strange. Very strange. "Fat people are more likely to have work-related accidents. Did you know that?" she says to me.

"No," I whisper. I didn't know that at all.

She starts to cry. "It was horrible. She got caught in a machine. Skinny people can slip out of things. Skinny people almost never get caught in machines."

I get it. When you're huge, you're a huge target. It's easier to shoot a bear than a sparrow. But Jeannie didn't die or anything, so I don't understand what the big deal is.

"If I came home and found that dog on any other day . . ." Her voice trails off. "Oh God. I don't want to be the fat lady anymore. I want my identity back. Skinny women can be funny or intelligent or *interesting*. Fat women are just fat. That's always the first word people come up with. I want to be me again, and it should not feel like such an uphill battle."

"It's true," I say honestly. "You don't act the way you used to act. Sometimes I think you want to live in a chocolate house, so you can eat all the furniture and get diabetes."

"You're right. You're absolutely right. And don't let anyone ever tell you that it's only what's inside that matters. Sometimes you *can* judge a book by its cover. That's what covers are for. People can take one look at me and know I'm angry, that I lack willpower, and that I don't try very hard. The extra weight I carry around isn't just on the outside anymore. It's starting to sink below the skin. I'm tired. I'm frustrated. I feel defensive and alone. I'm putting my heart and my joints through hell. And I'm one of the lucky ones. We're in the middle of a recession. I've got a good, strong job. What if I get hurt at work and can't support you? I missed your graduation because I wanted hamburger casserole. I'll never forgive myself for that. And Jeannie doesn't have kids. She doesn't know what it's like to be a single parent. I'm supposed to be bringing my A game."

I laugh, because hearing Mom say "A game" is ridiculous. She thinks I'm laughing at her in general.

"Go ahead. Laugh all you want. I tell you how I feel inside, because I trust you; you're my son. You're the man of the house now. When you laugh at me, it hurts."

I'm glad Charlie's not here, because I wrap my arms around Mom's doughy shoulders and say, "Don't cry, Mom. I wasn't laughing at you. I was laughing at something funny you said."

"I wasn't trying to be funny!"

"Mom, trust me. You talking about bringing your 'A game' is kind of funny."

She laughs a little bit. "I don't know where I picked that up. Maybe watching hockey."

I can smell her oatmeal-cookie soap. She starts crying uncontrollably, and I'm worried I've done the wrong thing, that somehow in hugging her I have made the situation worse, except that can't be true. I keep my arms wrapped tightly around her for a long time, until she stops trembling, until she's done crying. "It's gonna be okay," I tell her. "Everything's gonna be okay."

"I really don't like carrots," she whispers. "How am I supposed to do this?"

I notice the black fly isn't buzzing in our window anymore. It has found its way back out into the world.

"Dad taught me a way to fix carrots that's not so bad. I just need some cider vinegar and some garlic."

"I took your dog on a walk earlier. I think I'd like to walk him every morning, if it's okay with you."

So this is what it might feel like. A new beginning.

CHAPTER 24
CONFRONTATION

I have glass in my face. Or maybe it just *feels* like there's glass in my face. I'm lucky nothing got into my eyes, because last weekend, when Charlie destroyed part of the Freak Museum, he didn't care who got hurt. It was real stupid of us to show up at Cornpup's house, thinking we were gonna surprise him with our campout idea and an envelope full of Freak Tour money. We should've known he'd mutter some crap about how he can't get the surgery now, or ever, because Gramps has a bad heart and can't deal with the worry. We should've known he was gonna tell us to cancel the campout.

I should've known to grab Charlie's arm right then before he snapped.

Charlie looked so crazy, lifting jars of colored creek water above his head, one by one, and smashing them on Cornpup's hardwood floor. Red and green splattering on the walls. Slimy blue liquid dripping down the door. Orange stains on the bed. Grayish gel seeping into a floor vent. Creek water and twigs, dead bugs and tiny bones. Cornpup was shouting, "Stop it. I'm serious, stop it. I need those!" and I was standing in the middle of it all with a piece of glass in my face.

Now, a week later, we're setting up the campsite, and it's a chilly night, and there are still cuts under my eye.

I help Molly carry cases of pop from the car. She brought hot dogs, ice, bags of candy, and pretzel rods. She brought graham crackers and marshmallows and chocolate squares.

"The campsite looks awesome," she says, kissing Randy on the lips.

"I did most of it," says Charlie, and that's not the truth. It was me who helped Randy put the tent stakes in the ground while Charlie played with Viper in the creek.

But the fire is going strong, surrounded by sleeping bags and folding chairs, and there are lots of kids here now, raiding the cooler for soda. Valerie is here with me, so I feel real happy, like I don't care that Cornpup isn't coming.

I don't care about Cornpup at all.

Charlie and Jill collect money from the campers. Me and Val teach Viper to fetch a tennis ball. She tells me her brother really wants to meet me, that he might show up tonight if this other party he's going to gets raided by the cops. She tells me her little cousin Katie won't swim in the creek anymore because my goblin pee stories grossed her out.

"I wasn't trying to keep kids out of the creek," I say. "I would never do that."

"It's probably good if little kids don't swim there," Val says. "You did a good thing."

She is so unbelievably pretty, and I don't want to argue with her, so I change the subject. "I heard something about Kevin Thompson

163

showing up here tonight. Something about him wanting to fight me with a crowbar."

Valerie laughs. "Maybe that's him over there," she says, pointing to a shadow moving quickly through the industrial park. For a second, I think maybe it *is* Kevin. I watch the shadow move closer, until I hear baseball cleats crunching on a path of dry pine needles. I stand up, ready for a fight, ready to put a real end to this.

Cornpup steps into the firelight.

"I thought you weren't coming." I sit back down and relax my fists.

"Can we just not talk about this?" Cornpup says. He opens a bag of pretzels, sits down on a rock facing me and Val, and all of a sudden it's like we were never fighting, which is so weird.

Randy opens a scratched-up black guitar case.

Charlie is standing protectively over two cans of gasoline.

"What's that for?" I ask him. Because he and Randy built this fire with their hands.

"You're not gonna be the only celebrity tonight," he says. "I've got something planned. Something amazing."

Molly sits on a large tree stump. She rummages through the cooler, finds a Sprite, and pops the tab. She shakes water from her hand. "Help yourselves," she says to a group of shy little girls. "We have orange Crush, Mountain Dew, and some cola."

"You should take this now." Charlie passes an envelope to Cornpup. "Two hundred and twelve dollars." I see something in Charlie's eyes. He is saying *Good luck*.

Cornpup looks at the envelope for a long time. "I came here because you guys put a lot of work into this thing. But I'm still not having the surgery." He doesn't hand the money back to us, though. Instead he folds the envelope in half and tucks it into his back pocket. He will eventually go through with the surgery. It's so obvious.

Soon we are gathered around the campfire, crunching on potato chips like a bunch of termites. Randy strums his guitar. Molly collects candy wrappers and empty pop cans, and tosses them into a black garbage bag. Charlie hands out long, smooth sticks for roasting marshmallows.

But what the kids really came here for is me. I tell ghost stories like I'm on fire. I weave each tale into one of the original landfill legends, until I have built a complex web.

Valerie's looking at me. I can feel it.

The kids raise their hands and let me call on them like they're in school. They want to know what will happen when the aliens come back. They want to know what the world was like before the robot wars began. They want me to tell them why there's been so much demon diarrhea in the creek lately.

Cornpup says, "We all want to know the answer to that one."

Midnight comes and goes.

One by one, the youngest kids yawn and find their blankets. Randy plays an acoustic Audioslave song. He sings, "I am not your rolling wheels; I am the highway," and sounds exactly like Chris Cornell. I talk to Valerie for a while, but then I start feeling restless. I want to get away from Charlie and Jill, who are sitting a few feet away from us, kissing each other sloppily. They sound like dogs licking gravy off a plate.

"Nice camera," I say to Cornpup.

"I borrowed it from a librarian," he says. "It takes great night pictures. Feel like taking a walk?"

Valerie's eyes drop to her hands. I know she's disappointed. She wants to sit by the fire with me. She wants to hold my hand. I leave Viper behind to keep her company.

Away from the campfire, there is total darkness. I've always liked the sky best when it's the color of black paint and there's a crescent moon, all sharp, like a weapon. We walk along the banks of the creek. The water makes strange, gurgling sounds. Cattails brush our legs, and it makes me think of zombie hands, reaching up from the grave.

Cornpup says, "This is gonna sound weird, but I'm starting to *like* my messed-up skin. I wanted to look normal so bad, and now I actually have a way to get rid of all my cysts, and suddenly I feel like I should protect them. Because they're, like, a part of me."

"I felt like that the day of the Freak Tour," I tell him. "I felt like my stories were a part of me and I was giving them away too easily. Sometimes soldiers feel that way after getting shot. They don't want the doctors to remove the bullets. Maybe you can keep some of your cysts in a jar after the surgery, like how people keep their kidney stones."

Cornpup isn't listening. He is staring at the drainage pipes behind the Mareno Chem building.

"Look at this. They're *still* dumping. They're so cocky."

He snaps a picture of a few scattered windows that are glowing from within the warehouse. The camera flash is real bright. He takes about a hundred pictures of a Mareno Chem drainage pipe spewing dark, chunky sludge from its mouth. He takes off his shoes and wades into the creek. He snaps two head-on pictures of the drainage pipes with the Mareno Chem complex looming in the background. He steps out of the slimy water and uses his socks to wipe his feet clean. He puts his shoes back on, and we walk back to the campsite in silence. I sort of hear a third set of footsteps, but when I look back, I see only Cornpup, who is crazy with excitement. "Wait till the EPA sees these pictures. And the newspaper. And the cops."

A smooth, deep voice says, "Give me the camera."

Me and Cornpup freeze like animals in the line of fire. I feel a thick arm coil around my neck, securing me in a tight headlock.

"Let him go," Cornpup says calmly.

"I saw you from my office window, that bright flashing camera. Were you *trying* to get my attention?" I can't turn my head, but I recognize Dan Benecke's voice. When he talks, I feel pinpricks in my skin. He knows exactly who we are. He probably knew we'd come back out here sooner or later. Maybe he was waiting for us.

"Cornpup, run. Get Charlie." I try to shout. But Dan Benecke's arm is like a steel vise, tightening. He could snap my neck if he wanted to. I let out a pitiful cough. It's hard to breathe.

I can *feel* how bad Dan Benecke wants to kill us. He is tired of dealing with us. But I have to give him props. He is acting real calm. He says, "Hand me the camera, and you can both go home."

Cornpup snaps the most incriminating photo of all: Dan Benecke choking me. "Whoa. That one's gonna make the front page," he says, and snorts. "Now let go of my friend."

"I don't get you, kid. Why do you insist on being a pain in my ass? What is it with you and these drainage pipes?"

Cornpup snaps another picture. "Oooh. I think the cops'll really like that one," he says. "You look *dangerous*."

I tell Cornpup to please go get Charlie, but he doesn't move.

"Have you considered what you boys are doing to your community?" Dan Benecke asks us. "All I have to do is say the word, and Mareno Chem pulls out of Poxton. We move hundreds of jobs to Ohio. Is that what you want?" He tightens his grip on my throat. "Now hand over that camera, before you do some real damage."

"I'm not giving you this camera," Cornpup says.

Dan Benecke throws me to the ground. I look up at him and see the scar I created, a fault line on his face. He lunges for the camera, but Cornpup is too quick for him. It seems like we might win this round. Until I notice the white envelope under Dan Benecke's boot.

Cornpup's money.

Dan Benecke picks up the envelope. One look at our faces, and he knows he's got something we want. He says, "I'll give this back to you when you give me the camera."

Cornpup doesn't react.

"Just give him the camera," I whisper. "You can't screw up your skin over this. Seriously."

"Get up off the ground," Cornpup says to me. "And run!" He takes off, wheezing but fast, and I follow. Dan Benecke is at our heels. We know the terrain better than he does, but he is angry enough to keep a hungry speed.

"I don't have my inhaler," Cornpup says in a frightened voice.

"Don't think about it," I tell him. "Just breathe. We're almost there."

Through the trees I can make out our campfire. I see Randy laughing. I see Jill sitting next to Valerie, hovering close to the fire. They are all smiling. They don't know we're being chased by a madman. They don't know the Freak Tour money is gone.

When we reach the campsite, Cornpup collapses onto the ground.

"Find his inhaler," I say to Valerie. "It should be in his bag."

If this campfire wasn't here, if Randy and the others weren't loud and awake, Cornpup's lungs would've quit, and Dan Benecke would've caught us, and then . . . what?

Randy puts down his guitar and shouts at me. "What the hell happened? Why is Cornpup crying? Why are you holding your neck?"

The gasoline cans are gone.

"Where's Charlie?" I say.

Everyone looks at me blankly.

Where's Charlie? I say again, this time with panic in my voice.

"I don't know," says Randy. "I thought he went to find you."

We hear the explosion then. We feel the ground shake.

Randy looks at me. "Oh no," he says. "Oh shit."

CHAPTER 25
FIRE

FLAMES taller than trees. The sky full of green smoke. Fumes that taste like the apocalypse.

Mareno Chem is burning.

Me and Randy run. I don't know or care what the others do. I feel like I'm on fire, like my arms and face are frying.

Randy feels it too. "Chemical burns," he says to me. "Our skin'll be raw for the next few days." My lungs lock up like a seizing engine. We take off our shirts and use them to cover our mouths. The chemicals still penetrate our bodies, seeping through our pores. My eyes are watering so bad, it must look like I got pepper-sprayed.

"Charlie!" I shout. "This isn't funny. Where are you?"

The ground is choppy, with waves of dirt, like a stormy lake. Or maybe the ground isn't moving at all. Maybe I'm hallucinating. We use the trees to help us stand, and even then I feel motion sickness, like I'm on a boat. I think about strange things—slugs crawling up a windowpane, pelicans eating a pile of fingers, Randy with three arms and one eye.

We're oxygen deprived.

Mareno Chem is in front of us now, except I have no idea how we got here so fast. The parking lot is empty. Dan Benecke's Lexus is gone.

Spinning head. Foggy eyesight. Stomach won't stop twisting.

We call Charlie's name, but there's no answer.

I can't keep my eyes open. The burning is so bad. "I think someone poured acid into my eyes," I say to Randy. "Was someone just here?"

"What?" he says.

He doesn't understand the things that are coming out of my mouth, and neither do I.

I try to run toward the fire, to find Charlie, to save Charlie, but I fall. My legs aren't connected to my brain. I am wet bread, slices of cheese.

"I see him. Right there." Randy's eyes are watering like mine. He points to a shadow.

That's not Charlie. It's a bush.

"Where is he?" I am crying now. "Why isn't he coming out of the fire?"

Randy takes off his belt and uses it to fasten my T-shirt to my face. Randy is still sane enough to make me wear a homemade gas mask. "Get on the ground," he says. "Stay as low as you can. Crawl back to the campsite. Call a star bird. No. I don't know what I'm saying. Call an ambulance. Tell Molly and Cornpup to leave everything behind. Have them cover their mouths. Just get the kids to a safe place. Can you do that?"

He takes off his jeans and ties them around his face. A T-shirt isn't a thick enough filter, not for where he's going.

"Don't go into the fire," I say. "You'll die."

"Goddammit." Even with jeans covering most of his face, Randy still looks worried. "Just do what I told you."

I start crawling. My fingernails are full of dirt. I see a million worms, blink twice, and then the worms are gone. There's a sharp pain on the right side of my head, a fierce headache in a specific spot, but at least I can breathe again, sort of. The fumes aren't as bad down by the mud and weeds. Maybe I'll make it back to the campsite alive.

Please, Charlie. Be alive.

The sky is churning, a yellow gray with bits of stars peeking through heavy smoke. I have chemical blisters on the backs of my hands. I blink, hoping they'll go away like the worms, but the blisters are real. My skin is bubbling.

Your skin is an organ, Cornpup once said. *It can breathe. It can die.*

The campsite is already cleared out. Valerie and Jill have taken Viper and the campers back to Cardinal Drive. Cornpup went home to call 911 and get his gas mask for Molly, paper surgical masks for the rest of us. There are piles of vomit on some of the sleeping bags.

"It was so horrible. The kids all started puking." Molly is hyperventilating. "Where's Randy? Where's Charlie?"

I close my eyes. I was hoping Charlie might be here.

"Where *are* they?" Molly screams at me.

"Randy's looking for him." I can't even bring myself to say Charlie's name out loud. I start searching for him in stupid places. Behind the cooler. Under a blanket. Inside bags of chips. *What was he thinking?* I wonder. Why would he set a chemical plant on fire with two cans of gasoline? Not smart. Not smart at all.

Molly puts out the campfire with ice water from the cooler. "I can't leave without Randy."

We sit on rocks in the darkness, coughing and not speaking. Cornpup returns with a jug of water, which seems so dumb, because we're too freaked out to be thirsty. When he sees me and Molly are the only ones here, he looks away. He knows what I know: Charlie wouldn't mess with us for this long. Cornpup thinks it's all over now. He thinks Charlie's never coming back.

"Here," he says. "Use this water to wash out your eyes."

The Mareno Chem fire is raging, unstoppable. The sky is full of sirens and terrible colors. I have the most blisters, but Cornpup's skin is swelling. Molly's eyes are puffed up and orange, like dried apricots. We hear Randy before we see him.

"He sounds like he's crying. Doesn't he sound like he's crying?" Molly clasps her hands together and starts to pray so hard, I can see ugly green veins bulging from her neck. "Help us," she says over and over again. "Make Charlie be okay. Please."

"Stop it," Cornpup snaps. "Your God is a bully. Your God is sick."

Randy appears, wearing only boxer shorts and combat boots. He's holding Charlie, limp and gray, in his arms. *It's the chemicals. Making me see things. Charlie's skin isn't really gray. Everything is fine.* Molly jumps up and pulls the denim mask from Randy's face. She touches Charlie's cheek and jerks her hand away real quick. Her face turns phosphorus white. "You told me not to pray!" she shouts at Cornpup. "Are you happy now?"

Cornpup shouts back at her, "You can't blame me for this. I wasn't even here when Charlie left the campsite with two cans of gasoline. Why didn't you stop him?"

"Shut up," I say to both of them. "Just *shut* up. Charlie's fine. He's gonna be fine."

Randy is on his knees. He tries giving Charlie mouth-to-mouth, tries pumping his chest, but nothing changes. Charlie's body is like wax. Cornpup can't find a pulse.

"I don't understand," I whisper. "He didn't go into the fire. He didn't get burnt. Why isn't he okay?"

Randy says, "Where's the ambulance? I thought I told you to call an ambulance."

Cornpup says, "They're coming, but . . . Randy . . . it might be too late. I think it's too late."

"You don't know what you're talking about," Randy says, but his voice is shaky.

I vomit in the bushes, again and again, until the paramedics arrive, cup an oxygen mask over Randy's mouth, and zip Charlie into a bag.

No, I didn't see that. Charlie is okay. Charlie is invincible.

I wish someone would tell Molly to stop screaming.

The paramedics, the police, they're all talking at once:

". . . arson . . . tragedy . . . biggest fire I've ever seen . . . lots of questions . . ."

". . . he was standing too close to the fumes . . . fried his brain . . . Why are you kids out here?"

". . . warehouse is gone . . . evacuation . . . lucky they all aren't dead . . . blisters . . ."

". . . Don't these kids have parents? . . . chemicals . . . Is this the brother? . . . notify the family . . ."

". . . don't really know to what extent the fire is spreading . . . nerve damage . . ."

Randy says, "Get your hands off me. . . . What is wrong with you people? . . . doctors . . . Why didn't you even try to help him?"

I have dirt in my mouth. I can feel grit in my teeth. My right thumb is twitching, and I can't make it stop. Maybe this is my fault. I noticed the gas cans, but I didn't empty them in the grass. I could've saved him.

Flashing red lights. I pass out for a second and think of the lockbox Charlie gave me, how I wasn't supposed to open it, except I did open it, this morning, and there was nothing inside but a small horsehair paintbrush.

I am conscious again. I have an oxygen mask on my face. Someone puts me on a stretcher. I say, "I want to ride with Cornpup," but they don't know who Cornpup is.

I think of Charlie and his matches, Charlie and his fires, Charlie who hated safety gear, Charlie who hated weakness. I picture him standing close to those final flames, the furious heat, inhaling the fumes on purpose, deep breaths, feeling like a god. He went to sleep happy, invincible as far as he knew. And he left us the way he was meant to leave us, with sirens, a yellow sky, evacuations, and a punished, ruined chemical company smoldering on the horizon.

Charlie.

On the way to the hospital, I fall asleep in the ambulance. I dream that the industrial yards are lifting up, morphing into the shape of a giant monster. Factories bubble like warts on the monster's skin; dead trees grow in patches, like goblin fur; Two Mile Creek is a twisted spinal cord; Chemical Mountain is a single, all-seeing eye. The industrial monster has powerful breath, fumes that kill. We feel like people, but we're just little mites and fleas, living on the skin of a creature that is bigger than everything else we think we know.

CHAPTER 26
CHANGE

ON the night Mareno Chem shuts its doors for good, temperatures reach ninety-eight degrees, and the box fans in our windows are just making it worse, blasting hot air at our faces. Cornpup was supposed to be here at midnight. *Everyone* should be here by now. I sit in my driveway and lean against the garage door. With a piece of gravel, I draw uranium monster paw prints on the concrete. We have so much work to do. We have to get started real soon if we're gonna be done by sunrise.

I hear Cornpup before I see him. He's using a huge remote control to direct two of his robots. My favorite robot, the one we usually keep at the creek, has hidden compartments full of battle gear. The other, uglier robot needs to be oiled. It sounds all creaky and stiff. I laugh when both robots get stuck in the bushes and Cornpup has to pull them out. I hear him say, "Goddammit all to hell," because he has to put the newer robot's arm back on, and he can't get it to stay. When Cornpup and his lifelike hunks of junk finally roll up my driveway, he's picking twigs out of their aluminum joints, and sweating off all his glow-in-the-dark face paint.

"You got any of that left?" I ask him.

We mess with the glow-in-the-dark paint for about ten minutes. I smear tribal lines on my face, warrior-style. Cornpup paints the robots' faces to look all girly, with hilarious neon green eyeliner and lipstick.

"Paint something cool on my back," Cornpup says to me. He has been walking around shirtless, wearing the same pair of cargo shorts, since his surgery almost two weeks ago. We never got our envelope of cash back after Dan Benecke stole it, but Cornpup's parents finally gave in and bought him the detox tea and skin care products and whatever else Dr. Gupta said Cornpup needed. Now Cornpup's skin is part smooth, part craters and scars, and he's smiling so hard, I think his face might snap. When I look at his bony back, I remember exactly where the gray and purple rashes used to be. I remember how he used to have a mountain range of pus-filled monster cysts rising from his spine, all pale-white and chunky. Cornpup stands with his back to me, and I paint a glow-in-the-dark hawk on his skin. The hawk's wingspan stretches all the way across Cornpup's shoulder blades. It looks pretty cool.

I think of the funeral, how horrible it was, the throbbing blisters on our arms, Cornpup ripping out hymnal pages; Mrs. Pellitero with snot dripping down her lips; Mr. Pellitero passed out, snoring; Valerie holding my hand like I was drowning; and Randy, who could not control his anger, putting his fist through a stained-glass window and getting blue slivers stuck in his knuckles. I got really teary-eyed when Mom showed up carrying a big piece of poster board with pictures of us as boys taped all over it. She was crying. I could tell she was sorry for how mean she'd been to Charlie, how judgmental, except sorry is just a word, a feeling. When someone dies, sorry is kind of *meaningless*.

You have to do something really meaningful for the dead. It was instinct, the way we all silently agreed to send Charlie off like an Egyptian king that dreary morning. We filled the casket with stuff we thought he might somehow need—his monster mask, a silver rattlesnake ring, a jar of green creek water, his football helmet, a jackknife, bags of candy, letters sealed in envelopes, and my book of landfill mythology. Even Cornpup, who thinks the afterlife is bullshit, brought one of our dragon skeletons in a duct-taped box.

Charlie.

No one even knows what to call him now. He was a criminal, a vandal, an *arsonist*. When he destroyed Mareno Chem, he put good people out of work—machinists, systems operators, truckers, chemical technicians, assembly line workers—and it's not like there are a bunch of replacement jobs out there. But here's the thing: At the burial there were sick people; *dying* people; lines of pale, skinny, chemo-bald strangers. They brought flowers to Charlie's grave. They whispered, "Thank you." To them, he was a hero, somebody who fought back, a brave kid who'd chased the poison makers away. Charlie took back our neighborhood, our creek, our *territory*. It's not like people were pounding down Mareno Chem's door with a bunch of ridiculous demands. We just wanted them to stop messing with our lives.

In the cemetery, when a newspaper reporter asked me to comment, I wanted to say something about Dad, how Mareno Chem had stolen him from me, and how Charlie had carried out the sweetest revenge, but my throat was real dry. Cornpup spoke instead. He said, "Now the chemical companies have to listen to us. Now they can be afraid for once."

Me and Cornpup sit on my front porch, waiting for the others. I smell asphalt and burning sulfur in the air. Cornpup is wheezing lightly. I help him attach paint rollers to the robots' hands with duct tape. He then uses plastic wrap to cover the robots' exposed joints and gears, places where a stray drip of paint could do real damage.

I think about the evacuations, how scared everyone must've been, with the sky all yellow and green. I think about flashing lights, sirens. The night of the fire, emergency responders divided Poxton into three rings. The innermost ring was made up of all the homes closest to the industrial yard, our entire neighborhood. I was in the hospital when the evacuations were ordered, but Mom told me it happened in stages. Residents in the first ring had to put wet washcloths over their faces and leave immediately. Residents in the second ring could stay in their homes if they closed their chimney flues and sealed their windows with masking tape. Then, as the fire raged on and fumes blanketed every home in Poxton, even the mansions in the outer ring near Buffalo were contaminated. Mom said she was trying to get to the hospital to find out if I was okay. The streets were crowded with cars, everyone trying to leave town in a panic. She said the green smoke left a chalky soreness in the back of her throat. And Viper was drooling a lot, drinking tons of water. In the last couple of weeks, Mom has hugged me more than a thousand times. She is so glad I'm alive.

I hear music in the distance, probably a live band at Tavern on the Creek. Randy and Molly appear at the end of my driveway. They seem cheerful, which is saying a lot, considering what has happened to the Pellitero family in the past few weeks: Charlie's death, divorce paperwork, home foreclosure. Molly has on coveralls. Randy is carrying four large cans of paint. "What the hell are those for?" he says, meaning the robots.

"To help out," says Cornpup.

"They know how to paint?" Molly laughs.

Cornpup looks at her like she's truly stupid. "I wouldn't exactly say they know anything. They just do repetitive motions, basic stuff."

Inside my garage, there are two ladders we lifted from a nearby construction site. Randy helps me carry them outside. Molly pulls a box of dusty paintbrushes and rollers out from under Dad's workbench. None of us wants to carry my canvas bag of scrap metal, though. It's like we're now just remembering that we have to walk a really long way with all this stuff. Cornpup runs home to grab the shopping cart he found under a bridge at Two Mile Creek. It's not big enough to carry everything, but it'll help.

When I accidentally knock over my dirt bike, Randy flinches. I prop it up quickly, but he runs over to the bike and pushes me out of the way. He touches the shiny motor I just polished a few days ago. He touches the muddy tires. "When Charlie bought this for you, I thought he was nuts. Everything he did was always so . . . huge."

It never even crossed my mind that this bike might've been from Charlie. Except now, looking back, it makes sense. I remember him telling me he "lost" his football camp money at the creek that year, and it seemed like a bullshit story. Charlie didn't *lose* things, especially when it had to do with football.

Charlie.

Every time I feel like I'm moving past his death, I get thrown back into it. I wish we could all find a way to stop ripping off the scab.

After the funeral and long before the chemical blisters had healed, we took Cornpup's freshly developed Mareno Chem photos to the newspaper. The reporter spilled coffee down the front of his shirt, coughed a little bit, and said, "Are these for real?" He kept looking at a photo of Dan Benecke choking me. Finally he said, "This is front-page stuff. I hope you're ready, because you boys are about to start a shit storm." What followed were lawsuits and public outcry. Barbed-wire fences, government inspections, and tens of thousands of dollars in fines. Mareno Chem workers lined up outside the unemployment office. Chemical tankers were confiscated, barrels dug up, soil samples taken. Dan Benecke was arrested, charged with felonies. I wish we could've been there to see it. I would've stood in front of his mansion and shouted, *Hope they put you away forever, asshole! No more fancy vacations! And you can kiss your stupid Lexus goodbye!* It would've felt so good.

No one ever found the Phenzorbiflux, though. It has disappeared. And I'm not searching anymore.

Cornpup runs up my driveway with his shopping cart, but my attention is focused on Valerie and her brother, Matt, who've just arrived. Their dad works at a hardware store, and they weren't kidding when they said they could get their hands on cheap supplies. Val is pulling a wagon full of dented paint cans with no labels. She smiles at me, and I want to kiss her. Matt is carrying a jug of paint thinner, a box of broken glass, and an industrial-sized tub of plaster. His hair is spiked in a short Mohawk. He tells me about this party he's having next weekend.

"You should stop by," he says. "I want you to meet everyone before school starts. My friend Michiu is studying to be a filmmaker. He's really gonna dig your monsters."

"It'll be so much fun," Val says. "You have to come."

I manage to smile a little bit. It'll be cool to have some artist friends when school starts, even if they are a full year ahead of me. And it can't hurt to get in good with Valerie's brother. High school is still nipping at my heels, and Kevin Thompson is still roaming the neighborhood with his guns, and Charlie is forever gone. I try really hard to focus on the good things in my life. Mom is acting like her old self again, eating less. Cornpup is still here. I am meeting some new people. My girlfriend is unbelievably pretty. And Viper is the greatest dog ever.

We hike along Two Mile Creek with our art supplies, paint cans, and ladders. Cornpup presses the "forward" buttons on his remote controls. The robots follow him, struggling through the mud. Two

Mile Creek is quiet tonight—no bubbling, no sludge. When we reach the edge of the old Mareno Chem property, I swear I can feel Charlie laughing from somewhere deep in the sulfur-smelling sky.

The chemical complex is in ruins. There are melted steel beams, piles of blackened rubble, chemical tanks, smoking and oozing.

Molly touches her fingertips to a towering wall of concrete. "This building looks almost like a skeleton now. It's so weird how this is the only wall that didn't burn."

We start slowly. It takes time to get a feel for the brushes in our hands, to set up our flashlights and lanterns, to figure out what colors are in the unlabeled cans. I paint detailed outlines of my monsters, lifelike in size, terrifying. Valerie adds webs of burnt trees to the background. Cornpup's robots use rollers to paint a yellow and green chemical sky. With epoxy, Matt attaches broken glass to the monsters' bodies for texture. Molly stands high on a ladder and paints a ball of flames where the moon should be. Randy sculpts fangs and jagged bones out of plaster. I add tiny details: black blood oozing from the petroleum serpents' injuries; a two-headed squirrel on the shores of our creek; and the fault line, with Chemical Mountain looming in the distance. Cornpup adds one detail of his own. He covers the uranium monster in hideous purple rashes and white, pus-filled cysts. All of us, we paint with madness, a fire in our guts.

At sunrise, we want to take a break. We want to step away from the wall so we can get a good look at our work. The robots are out of juice, and our flashlights are out of batteries, and we're as hungry as hell, but still, we keep painting. We only stop once, briefly, to watch what must be a hundred birds circling a nearby landfill. It starts out as just a few seagulls, black silhouettes against the rising sun. Then the sky starts to spin with layers of gulls and vultures and hawks. It feels like the birds are here for us, like they're putting on a show.

Randy says, "Why do they keep circling that thing? They can't get to the garbage. It's buried."

"They can get to the rats," Valerie whispers, and I smile because this past summer, me and Charlie and Cornpup were like birds of prey. We brought Mareno Chem to its knees.

We got to the rats.

For another hour, we work. We cannot quit until Charlie's wall is perfect. We've got a rhythm down: telling funny stories, laughing, singing, flinging globs of paint at each other. In some ways, it's the best night of our lives. We're declaring victory over Mareno Chem. We're painting this tribute to Charlie. We are bonded in creativity and insomnia.

When the pink sunrise gives way to real daylight, we pack up our gear. We stare at our wall of monsters for a long time, taking in every detail, every bold brush of color, such terrifying beauty. This monster mural is the most amazing thing any of us has ever been a part of. It looks like it was done by famous artists, not a bunch of regular kids from Poxton. I open up Charlie's lockbox, and I pull out the horsehair paintbrush he gave me. One by one, quietly, we say our goodbyes. I say goodbye to Charlie. I say goodbye to Dad. I say goodbye to the anger that has been with me for too long. Then we take turns dipping the brush into green paint, signing our names boldly underneath the uranium monster's webbed feet.

Acknowledgments

Without a resplendent supporting cast, I'd be a neurotic hermit buried under an avalanche of unfinished manuscripts. My *Chemical Mountain* exists because of the wonderful people in my life:

My wise, generous, patient, handsome, and accomplished husband. Thank you for taking me on adventures, supporting all my dreams, always knowing just what to say, and being the person I rely on most of all. You are the love of my life.

My gentle-hearted grandmother. You always walked me to the library, allowed me to linger, helped me carry home stacks of books, and then read to me tirelessly, even when the Cubs game was on. Thank you for introducing me to the world of literature. I don't go a minute without missing you.

My lioness mother, who is fearless and beautiful. Thank you for teaching me to view the world through an artist's eyes, for showing me how to question the status quo, for treating all my creative endeavors like masterpieces, and for loving me no matter what. I'm so lucky to be your daughter.

My little brother (who is much taller than me now). Thank you for diffusing all my nebulous worries, cracking me up when I get too serious, always being available when I need to go out for cupcakes, and letting me dress you up in wacky outfits when we were kids. You've given the gift of joy to everyone who knows you, especially me.

My bright, darling son, the child of my dreams, magnificent in every way. You were with me through the revisions and when I mailed this manuscript off to my publisher. You fill my life with laughter, Matchbox cars, and sweet moments. My love for you is endless. You said it best: "Mom-mom's happy because she's with her boy."

Dad, who saved every drawing, every story. Kathy, who understands all things Pisces and is an excellent confidante. Sandy, who is vigorously supportive. Parry, who rescues animals with tireless compassion. You have each given me love and encouragement in spades, and I am so grateful.

My loyal, fabulous, and beautiful girlfriends, some of whom have been by my side since childhood, and all of whom are strong, fun, intelligent, brave, unique, and kind. Thank you for cheering me on and for being there. You are my sisters. Special thanks to Rhonda Hulpiau, who took me to see the landfills.

My critique group friends who helped me whip this book into shape, especially Robyn Gioia, Elle Thornton, Gregg Golson, Cynthia Enuton, and Janet Walter from the Jax novel group; Shelley Koon for rocking my author photo; Linda Bernfeld for making SCBWI Florida sparkle; Alvina Ling for early insights on character; Katie Burke for turning me on to the Left Coast Writers; and Danielle Morgera for being my first reader.

Françoise Bui, my talented, eloquent, and marvelous editor. I won't ever forget the shock and excitement of that first phone call. Thank you so much for choosing my manuscript and shaping this book, and for all the behind-the-scenes things you've done that I don't even realize. This book sparkles because of you.

Joyce Sweeney, my mentor, for all the advice, nurturing, and tireless support. Without you, I would've been lost. The bean ceremony was one of the highlights of this whole journey. You are a wonderful teacher and a dear friend. I'm honored to be your number 32.

Tina Wexler, difficult-to-please wielder of the red pen, steadfast nurturer of fragile confidence. You rescued me from the netherworld of slush. You helped me grow as a writer. You are my friend and guiding star. Thanks for challenging me when I needed it most.

All of the extraordinarily talented people at Delacorte Press who've played a part in transforming my manuscript pages into this breathtaking book, especially Shane Rebenscheid and Kenny Holcomb for the perfect, amazing cover art and design, and Bara MacNeill and Colleen Fellingham for the meticulous copyediting. You are deeply appreciated.

SCBWI for the endless inspiration, enrichment, and professional guidance. There is something magical about being immersed in a culture of writers and illustrators who create works of art for children and teens. A special thank-you to Lin Oliver and Steve Mooser for creating the SCBWI family.

And last but certainly not least, thank you to all the librarians, human rights activists, artists, environmental stewards, musicians, book lovers, and fellow writers out there. You make the world a better place.

About the Author

Corina Vacco felt compelled to write about toxic towns after reading an article alleging that hundreds of thousands of children and teens throughout the United States attend schools built on or near dangerously polluted sites. She found the inspiration for this book while living in western New York, where she heard teachers speak out against a landfill adjacent to an elementary school.

A city girl, world traveler, and activist, Corina enjoys playing guitar, listening to the blues, and exploring the great outdoors. She lives in Berkeley, California, with her husband, who is a member of the U.S. Coast Guard, and their magnificent puddle-splashing, car-loving little boy. They share their home with one slightly neurotic but very lovable Italian greyhound and a growing collection of books. *My Chemical Mountain* is Corina's first novel. You can share your pollution-inspired stories, poetry, or artwork with her on mychemicalmountain.com.